CONQUEST

What Reviewers Say About Ronica Black's Work

In Too Deep

"*In Too Deep*, by newcomer Ronica Black, is emotional, hot, gripping, raw, and a real turn-on from start to finish, with characters you will fall in love with, root for, and never forget. A truly five star novel, you will not want to miss…"—*Midwest Book Review*

"Ronica Black's debut novel *In Too Deep* has everything from non-stop action and intriguing well-developed characters to steamy erotic love scenes. From the opening scenes where Black plunges the reader headfirst into the story to the explosive unexpected ending, *In Too Deep* has what it takes to rise to the top. Black has a winner with *In Too Deep*, one that will keep the reader turning the pages until the very last one."—*Independent Gay Writer*

"Black's characterization is skillful, and the sexual chemistry surrounding the three major characters is palpable and definitely hot-hot-hot…if you're looking for a solid read with ample amounts of eroticism and a red herring or two you're sure to find *In Too Deep* a satisfying read."—*L Word Literature*

"…an exciting, page turning read, full of mystery, sex, and suspense."—*MegaScene*

"…a challenging murder mystery—sections of this mixed-genre novel are hot, hot, hot. Black juggles the assorted elements of her first book with assured pacing and estimable panache."—*Q Syndicate*

Wild Abandon

"Black is a master at teasing the reader with her use of domination and desire. Emotions pour endlessly from the pages, moving the plot forward at a pace that never slows or gets dull. But Black doesn't stop there. She is intent on giving the reader more... Black's first novel *In Too Deep* is a finalist for a 2005 Lammy and for two GCLS awards. With *Wild Abandon* the author continues her winning ways, writing like a seasoned pro. This is one romance I will not soon forget."—*Just About Write*

"The sophomore novel by Ronica Black is hot, hot, hot."—*Books to Watch Out For*

"If you enjoy complex characters and passionate sex scenes, you'll love *Wild Abandon*."—MegaScene

Hearts Aflame

"Sleek storytelling and terrific characters are the backbone of Ronica Black's third and best novel, *Hearts Aflame*. Prepare to hop on for an emotional ride with this thrilling story of love in the outback... Wonderful storytelling and rich characterization make this a high recommendation."—*Lambda Book Report*

"*Hearts Aflame* takes the reader on the rough and tumble ride... The twists and turns of the plot engage the reader all the way to the satisfying conclusion."—*Just About Write*

Deeper

"This sequel to Ronica Black's debut novel, *In Too Deep*, is an electrifying thriller. The author's development as a fine storyteller shines with this tightly written story. ...[The mystery] keeps the story charged-never unraveling or leading us to a predictable conclusion. More than once I gasped in surprise at the dark and twisted paths this book took."—*Curve Magazine*

Visit us at www.boldstrokesbooks.com

By the Author

In Too Deep

Deeper

Wild Abandon

Hearts Aflame

Flesh and Bone

The Seeker

Chasing Love

Conquest

CONQUEST

by
Ronica Black

2011

CONQUEST

ISBN 10: 1-60282-229-8
ISBN 13: 978-1-60282-229-0

This Trade Paperback Original Is Published By
Bold Strokes Books, Inc.
P.O. Box 249
Valley Falls, NY 12185

First Edition: June 2011

CREDITS
EDITOR: CINDY CRESAP
PRODUCTION DESIGN: SUSAN RAMUNDO
COVER DESIGN BY SHERI (GRAPHICARTIST2020@HOTMAIL.COM)

Acknowledgments

Thank you, Bold Strokes Books, as always, for supporting me and taking this book on. Thanks to my editor Cindy and to all those at BSB behind the scenes, much love and gratitude to you all.

Dedication

For passion. For sex. For love. And always, for C.

CHAPTER ONE

What Jude Jaeger sought was simple. What she needed, complicated. Woman. She had at least one a night, sometimes two. And she gave them what no one else could or would. The ability to scream, to beg, to cry. To come.

Making women come was her drug of choice and she was so addicted it was like air to her now. She breathed it in and out as she walked the dimly lit club to seek out another. The dark walls pulsed around her, throbbing with the powerful industrial beat. The music was there to encourage their heartbeats, to push their adrenaline onward and forward, and to mask their cries of pleasure. She felt like a hunting animal moving through it, with no need for words. Heated glances, intense stares, and eager touches sufficed.

She grew excited as she considered the night ahead. Would it be another regular tonight, or would it be a virgin? She liked to call them "pretenders of innocence," and she could recall quite easily what it had felt like when she'd been one not all that long ago.

She'd been shy and lanky, a young woman from a different country, freshly slaughtered from her first and last relationship. She needed a place to unwind, a place safe from things like commitment, love, expectations, and emotion. And she was curious about things that were unspeakable to most. She'd lurked there in the corner of the club one stormy night, her hair dripping cold drops of rain onto her bare shoulders. She was hoping no one would notice her but secretly dying inside for someone to. She remembered the fear. The excitement. The quick onset of hot lust as she'd openly watched two women nearly tear themselves apart in a frenzy of fucking. What tiny morsel of innocence she'd had at that moment had fled. It ran down her body like heavy water and snaked right out the door. What replaced it was need. The need to watch. The need to touch. The need to take.

Because no one was ever really innocent. Not there.

And the virgins came by the dozen. Men, women. Lots of women. Curious, excited, anxious, aroused. Soccer moms, housewives, business executives, and Bible school teachers. Jude got them all, and they weren't afraid to tell her all about their lives, especially during the first few minutes when their nerves were frayed and exposed and they weren't sure what to do with themselves. They'd talk and talk until she had them alone and pressed up against the wall for a hot, long kiss. Then the subject would shift to her. They'd want to know her name, where she was from, was she married, how many women she'd had.

But names were dangerous and, for the most part, meaningless. They were for places like the market or work or saying hello to the next door neighbor. They weren't for her. And they weren't for this place either.

She'd center their attention by kissing them long and hard and staring deep into their eyes. She'd calmly tell them what she wanted them to do. Then she'd help them by kissing their trembling hands, tracing their inner wrists with her tongue, and nibbling the delicate skin on their perfumed necks. They were hers in seconds, burning fiercely aroused gazes into her eyes, experiencing feelings many of them had never felt before.

Those feelings were what kept them all returning to the dimly lit club night after night, week after week. There was no better place in which such desires could be carried out. Not homes, not cars, not alleyways downtown. No. No other place would do as well as this unassuming black building with its private rooms and private doings. It contained them all, encouraged them all. Providing them a protective shroud for the deeds they dared do.

Dirty little fantasies. Dirty little deeds.

But the place was quiet now. Darkness had yet to completely settle outside. The evening sun still slanted lightly upon those that were lingering nearby, spotlighting their every move. As soon as the sun set, though, the lingerers would gravitate toward the building, free to move in the fading light, throwing cautious glances over their shoulders as they pushed through the door.

Jude pictured them as she stepped into her private room and closed the door. Even though she'd arrived a little early tonight, she didn't have much time. Quickly, she slipped off her slacks, blouse, and undergarments and folded them neatly. She put them in her duffel bag and then pushed it under the large bed. Her leather pants and vest were already laid out on the comforter, awaiting her. They felt cool as she slid into them, the soft leather lightly kissing her bare skin. She wanted to moan. The sensation was arousing.

After holding her eyes closed briefly to refocus, she opened them and took in the room. It was cozy but just spacious enough not to feel stifling. Every detail of it was her doing, from the mirrors on the ceiling to the different sources of light, to the well-stocked dresser against the wall. As efficient as it was, she made sure it felt warm and inviting as well. Women were all about ambience, and they wanted to feel comfortable and safe. Her first time had been in this room, but it had been cold and sterile, and when it became hers she'd made a note then and there to change it.

Her masculine cologne stung her neck in a long, cool spray while she studied her reflection and then finger-styled her hair. She flexed her jaw and noted the determined glint to her eyes. Nothing else mattered now. Nothing but this place and this room and those that she led into it.

Completely ready, she left the room to head toward the bar for her nightly drink. Two men she was familiar with were already seated there wearing leather attire, noses in their glasses. She walked tall and strong, and when she looked into their eyes they looked away. No one spoke. No one dared. The men especially. She had nothing to do with them, and that fact was clear, so clear they didn't dare speak to her or even look her in the eye. The bartender, a man she knew only as Cord, was the only one who did look her in the eye, and even that was only on occasion. He slid her a double shot of vodka and she wondered again what the night would bring in. A few other regulars? Pretenders of innocence?

She downed her drink and breathed deeply.

Two other familiar forms entered from the back hallway as she slid her empty glass along the bar. She knew one of them intimately and they both moved toward her now, hoping for her interest. But tonight and every night lately, she wanted to wait it out, anxious for those that might come through the front door. It opened as if on cue and another regular entered.

The day was dying. Twilight was here.

The lingerers would be coming soon.

Chapter Two

Mary Brunelle turned off the engine to her Chevy Aveo and sat for a moment trying to still her racing heart. Her destination was directly ahead, a building that appeared black and small from the front but extended further in the back, nearly hitting the block fence surrounding the deserted lot.

Shit.

She was there. Already. Why couldn't the drive have lasted a little longer? Why couldn't she have gotten lost?

A hot nervousness beat inside her just as it did before every other social encounter she had to endure. It didn't matter if she was arriving at work in the morning, entering the break room at lunch, or waiting in line at the post office after work. People made her nervous. There was no rational reason why. Not really.

Most people left her alone and let her go about her business. Her co-workers, on the other hand, were a bit of a different story. They stared (what she considered staring), sometimes made faces, whispered, and giggled behind her back. They made her feel exposed and awkward.

And yet, here she was. Meeting them at this club after work. In the downtown part of downtown.

But today was different. Her co-workers had *invited* her, specifically requesting she come. They said the club was mysterious and entertaining. A real must-see. Something they'd all enjoy. They'd have drinks and shoot the shit. Get to know Mary. Why didn't she ever go out with them?

The friendly banter had been seductive, pulling her in, speaking to that part of her that wanted so badly to be included. She hated that part of herself, knowing that the need and desire for acceptance could be dangerous. It was, after all, the reason she was there arguing with herself inside her car.

She eyed the club through her windshield. The building was like a dark abscess in the grayish light of dusk. There was no movement near or around it. Only a dozen or so cars were in the lot, sitting silently, telling her nothing. The overhead streetlights came on, glowing faintly, as if they didn't get enough power to actually work. She stared up at one and counted off the seconds while she deliberated her next move.

She should go in. Force herself to be social. Have a drink or two to drown her nerves. Just relax and, well, shoot the shit as they said.

No. She shook her head.

What she should do is go home and watch a good show over a bowl of Orville Redenbacher's. Feign a stomachache tomorrow at work when they asked why she didn't show.

But she wasn't a good liar. And they'd only keep asking until she gave in.

"Fuck it." She crawled from her car, shouldered her purse, and stood in the lot, staring at the front of the building. Her mind was still in the car, still trying to convince her to go home. She took advantage and walked quickly, breathing deeply through her nose. A red sign sizzled near the all-black door, the word *Conquest* singeing into her corneas again and again.

The door opened, startling her. A heavy wave of music thumped out just before a man did. He was husky and wearing all black, melting right into the building and the growing darkness. As he passed the blinking sign she saw the reflection of leather covering his body. A black studded hat sat snugly on his shaved head and sweat glistened on his neck and near his ears. He stopped at the edge of the building and lit a cigarette. The glow of it showed that he was watching her. Her mind caught up to her then and her throat tightened with fear.

What the hell was this place? Was this why her co-workers were so amused? Or worse, were they actually into this sort of scene?

Her car called to her in the comfort and safety of the encroaching darkness. She imagined crawling back inside and releasing a sigh of relief as she started the engine.

But no. That dangerous need for inclusion and acceptance forced her to remain. She looked at the business card she pulled from her slacks.

It said *Conquest* and had a simple one-line address. Yes, this was the correct place. She turned it over where her co-worker Carla Meeker had written in ink.

Don't be late, first drink on me!

She sank the card into her pocket and wiped her palms on her pants. The leather man inhaled gluttonously and smiled at her as he exhaled smoke through his nose.

"Nice night, ain't it?" he said, crossing one large black-booted foot over the other.

"Mm hm."

"You sure you're in the right place?" he asked, smiling like he knew a secret she didn't.

"I think so."

He didn't respond. Just kept smiling. It made her uncomfortable and she hurried toward the door. As she pulled it open she gave him one last glance and saw the pale, half moon sliver of his bare ass against the building. It added more fuel to her already raging bonfire of anxiety, and she tripped as she entered, a little afraid the man was going to give chase.

She blinked in the dim light as the throb of music beat against her chest like an angry fist. It wasn't as loud as it was powerful. Like a heavy heartbeat coming from the walls to slip into her skin and settle in her body, beating within her bones. Her body was a part of the club now. It had taken only seconds.

She stepped further in and realized the room was lit in black light where everything white glowed brightly. The most notable was the white light lining the bar. She searched the bodies slumped there on the barstools, took in their leather garb, and glanced away from the whites of their curious eyes. She imagined her co-workers sitting at a corner booth hidden in the darkness, laughing hysterically at her as she ambled around nearly blind.

But she didn't see any booths. Or tables. There was just a bar with several stools and a few wiry looking chairs placed near the corners of the room. Bodies seemed to birth from the wall, moving toward her with silent intent. They were cloaked in black, camouflaged like darkly shrouded soldiers on a ninja's mission. She struggled for courage. The bartender, resting two beefy bare arms on the bar, called out to her.

"This club is members only," he barked.

"I—" She fished out the card and searched for her voice. "I'm supposed to meet someone here." She held out the card and it trembled in her fingers.

She inhaled sharply, her senses on high alert, and she caught the slightly dank scent of the place. It smelled like maybe beer had been spilled on the industrial carpet. She shivered even though the club was comfortably warm.

The person from the wall was now directly next to her with Mary's card in hand. With an athletic build and slicked back short hair, Mary couldn't tell if the person was a man or a woman. All she saw was the glow of teeth blazing under the black light.

"Uh…hello," Mary said, a little uneasy at their close proximity. The person didn't answer and another one, this one wearing a mask that reminded Mary of Zorro, arrived at her side. She appeared to be female, shorter in stature with delicate looking cheekbones.

Mary expected them to speak, but instead they both moved in and began kissing her arms. A jolt shot through her as their hot, slick tongues registered, making their way up to her shoulders. Insistent hands palmed her hips and tried to drift up under her blouse.

"Oh my God. What—" She pushed on them. "What are you doing?" What the fuck was happening? What was this place?

"I think there's been some kind of mistake." Her heart threatened to leap out of her throat as body-racking fear overcame her.

She stumbled backward, but they moved with her, nimble fingers shoving upward on the short sleeves of her blouse, making way for the seeking tongues and sucking lips. She trembled again. This time with shock and fear and a deep, dark spark of lust trying to catch flame.

Panic came along with the burn of embarrassment. The people at the bar were staring. Not just staring but watching. Intently.

"I really think—" She started but couldn't finish. She'd never been touched like this. Ever. Not by one person, and certainly not by two. She was terrified, the whole situation indescribable and insane. But her skin was coming alive beneath their mouths and her eyes were threatening to close with pleasure, ready to cave in to it.

"She's so fresh. So so fresh," the smaller stranger said.

They groaned, their mouths devouring her shoulders like dogs tenderizing a tasty bone.

"Yes, let's take her back—"

Mary forced open her eyes, the words slamming reality home. What the fuck was she doing? What was wrong with her? She needed to run. And fast.

She pushed them away, her fear suddenly in control. "I have to go."

But they were back on her like magnets on metal, their glowing eyes alive and hungry.

"I have to go," Mary insisted. Where the fuck was Carla and everyone else? She grew angry, realizing they'd probably set her up. The joke was on her.

The strangers continued to paw at her, their hands clingy and determined, sticking to her like an overgrown jungle of Cat's Claw.

She turned and caught sight of the door, lit only by a dim Exit sign hanging above it. She wanted to cry out, to yell for help. But she knew she'd seem ridiculous and she was already embarrassed enough.

"Noooo," the strangers said, pulling her back. They laughed like evil little devils as they toyed with her. The laughter echoed in Mary's ears, and she felt like she was caught in a twisted nightmare or a strange Stanley Kubrick film. She couldn't escape.

Oh God.

"Nein."

The voice was low and strong, booming over the music. The laughter of the strangers ceased and their clingy hands fell from her body.

"But she's so—" the smaller one tried to say.

"Nein!"

Mary jerked at the power of the voice and felt the two strangers hurry away from her. The air felt empty around her and her skin tingled where their mouths had been. She hugged herself and felt a warm hand settle on her shoulder. She turned, curiously calm and somewhat eager to see who the voice belonged to.

Her breath caught in her chest.

She stared for a long moment, taking in the robust form with an angular face and razor sharp cheekbones. A knot of muscle flexed at the base of her jaw as the woman clenched her teeth.

Wicked gold eyes held Mary's gaze, flicking like crinkled foil in the sun, offset by a swatch of white-blond hair.

The woman was dressed like the others—a black leather vest and black leather pants. A hint of cleavage perspired at the opening of the vest. Her muscles were hard and marbled under the tanned, glowing skin of her arms. She was sleek and strong and, dear Jesus Christ, sexy.

"Come."

Mary wasn't sure she heard correctly. The word was said with an accent so heavy it seemed to weigh down the air in the room and press against her crotch. She squeezed her legs together, the rush of blood there sudden and overwhelming.

Oh fuck. I'm gay. I'm so gay.

She'd always had her secret crushes and attractions, but she'd never admitted it to herself. Now it was impossible to ignore or shove aside. It was raging in her head and in her body with every quick, cumbersome beat of her heart.

"I—"

But the woman silenced Mary with a fingertip pressed firmly to her lips.

"Come." She grabbed Mary's hand and tugged on her to follow. Saying no was not an option. Mary knew it, and it seemed everyone else did as well. The people at the bar turned back to their drinks, and the two strangers that had come at her from the wall were nowhere to be seen.

Mary stumbled along after the woman, not attempting to argue, not *wanting* to attempt to argue. She had no idea why she was following her, but a part of her felt safe and shielded, as well as a bit starstruck by her looks. The realization almost made her giggle with nerves.

They entered a long hallway and hurried past two doors on the right and two doors on the left. One had a window flanking the door, and inside, a man was tied to a large black cross. Two people dressed in leather were flogging him much to his apparent enjoyment.

Mary stumbled again, more nervous than ever. The woman squeezed her hand as if in reassurance and Mary followed her into the room at the end. The door had a hanging sign and Mary watched as the woman slid a rectangular piece of red into the cardboard frame. Green was on the other side. Stop and go. Her anxiety grew as they entered the room.

A large, flat bed was lit by two small lamps on end tables burning with blue bulbs. Another standing lamp with a red bulb was hidden behind the door. The red light collided with the dim blue light as the woman closed the door and leaned against it.

Random observations flooded Mary's mind. Purple. Blue and red make purple. Technically, the light in the room should now be purple. Again, Mary almost laughed with nerves. She forced herself to swallow, her heart thudding in her throat.

"What is this place?" she asked. She had to hear it. Had to know for certain what she'd already agreed to thus far by going back with her.

"I think you know," the woman said.

German. The accent was German. Mary was almost certain.

"No, I really don't. I was supposed to meet some frie—" She stopped short of calling them friends. "Some colleagues from work. Have you seen them? There should've been about six—"

"Let us talk about you," the woman interrupted her. "Your friends are not here."

"They could be in another room maybe?" Doing what? Having an orgy? "Is there like a party room or something? For groups."

The woman's laughter was throaty and sexy.

"Your friends are not here."

"Oh. Well, maybe I should—"

"You are here."

"Yes. But—"

"You had the card."

Mary blinked. "They gave me the card—"

"Then you are where you belong."

Mary wasn't sure what to say. The room was cozy and inviting, luring her in. It smelled of something exotic, something she couldn't place. Whatever it was, it was both stirring and comforting, encouraging her to remain. They were alone, after all. All alone in the blue and red light. No one could see. No one would know. Unless her colleagues planned this. Set her up. Even paid for it. She began to panic again.

"Did someone tell you about me? Did they pay for this?"

The woman's face showed confusion. "Nobody pays. Not with money."

Mary laughed nervously. "Did someone tell you about me?" "No."

Mary thought of the man down the hall. "Are you going to tie me up?" Oh God. The thought nearly made her crumble. It excited her.

The woman's response splintered her further. She pushed off from the door and touched Mary's face with the back of her hand. Her eyes seemed wolf-like. Like danger and power were trying to shine out from behind the raw beauty.

"I might."

"I'm…not sure."

The woman smiled. "I know."

"What's your name?" Mary asked.

"Here I don't have a name."

"No. Your real name." She stared into her eyes. "Please."

"What is yours?" Her hand lowered, tracing down to Mary's neck, the fingers playing with her hair.

"Mary."

The woman threw her head back and laughed again, deep and resonant. Sexy. The tendons in her neck moved, and Mary had a sudden urge to trace them with her tongue. The thought must've been written on her face because the woman caught her gaze and pulled her closer, her smile eaten up by a look of desire.

"Mary," she said like it was the most delicious word in the world. She kissed her hard, pushing into her lips with a painfully wonderful strength. Mary moaned in surprise and then in bliss as the woman held her tightly and began to move her lips more purposefully, capturing Mary's in wet, hot tugs and pulls. Mary groaned and gripped the woman's vest for dear life. She was so soft and supple and so damn warm. When she felt her tongue come, a hot current shot through her, weakening her knees, bringing her to her tiptoes. She clung to her helplessly as the tongue teased, lightly pushing just inside her lips, all sweet and slick, a sleek muscle of velvet darting inside her.

When her tongue came fully, Mary could no longer stand. She hung off her, desperate, helpless, hot. A limp, burning doll, begging to be positioned and played with.

"You want this," the woman said, whispering into her ear. "You want me."

Mary closed her eyes and swam in the throb of desire rushing through her.

"Mm hm," was all Mary could muster.

The woman lifted her with ease and shoved her against the wall. Mary's wrists were then pinned above her head.

"I'm going to make you come," the woman said.

Mary stifled a cry as the furnace-like lips found her jaw and an extremely tender part of her neck. Blood pounded between her legs.

What was happening? Was this happening? Oh yes, it was. And it was really fucking something else. Her eyes rolled back in her head and her toes curled inside her flats.

"I'm going to make you come," the woman said, this time stopping to look into Mary's eyes. "Hard." Her jaw tensed and Mary yearned for it, wanted to suck on the small straining wad flexing at the base.

"What's—" She was losing control. She was in a speeding car going downhill and she could no longer reach the pedals. Faster and faster and faster. Rationality raced by at an unrecognizable speed. She grasped for it, felt it sliding through her fingers. "I don't know what I'm feeling."

The woman released one of Mary's wrists then trailed her hand slowly down Mary's blouse to her slacks where she quickly unbuttoned and lowered the zipper. Before Mary could protest, she slid her hand inside and stroked her bare flesh with her long fingers.

"Uh—oh!" Mary tensed and clung to her with her free hand. It felt so good. So impossibly good.

"This," the woman said, "is how you feel." She leaned in and bit Mary's neck. Mary cried out, the sensation piercing and then warming. "You feel good. Wet. Excited. Do you feel good, Mary? Does this feel good?"

Mary nodded and caught her breath. "Mm hm."

The fingers stroked up and down, sliding within her flesh. Mary struggled to breathe, completely overwhelmed with pleasure. The woman was staring into her eyes, watching her face contort and crumple in ecstasy. Mary could see herself in her eyes, and for once, she didn't worry about what she looked like.

"Tell me what you are thinking," the woman said, slowing her fingers to a heavier, more intense motion.

Mary shook with awakening nerves. "I—I'm not sure."

"No?" She squeezed her fingers together, holding Mary captive by her most sensitive spot.

"I mean yeah. I—I feel good." She was speechless and trapped in the most desirable of confines. It made her feel raw and hypersensitive, like an animal in the wild, in tune with everything. She licked her lips and tried to focus. She felt the cool sweat on her brow and the hot slickness between her legs. Her body was gone, free from her control. And it was at the mercy of a stranger.

"You feel good?" The woman was serious yet toying with her. Mary could see it in the way her lips turned up on one side.

"Yes."

"What about now?" The fingers squeezed tighter and moved up and down slowly. Mary bumped her head against the wall and nearly bit her lip it was so good.

"Ye—yes!"

"Does it feel good, Mary?" She moved faster. "Does it? Tell me."

"Oh God, it does." She closed her eyes. "It does."

The woman laughed and kissed her way to the other side where she bit some more.

"Ah, fuck," Mary whispered.

"Do you want me to stop?" she asked, lightly kissing her lips.

"Huh? No." Mary shook her head.

"No?"

"No. Don't stop."

"Do you want to come?"

"Yes." More than anything. Mary wanted to come in this woman's arms, looking into her gorgeous face, pulsing against her powerful fingers. "I do."

The woman stared at her for a long, hard moment. Her eyes flicked with her thoughts. And then she stilled her hand and pulled away. Mary nearly sank to the ground, catching herself by pressing her palms back against the wall. They squeaked as she shoved herself into a full stand.

"What happened? Why—" She swallowed against her dry throat. "Why did you stop?"

The woman was moving around the room as if Mary weren't there at all, retrieving some things from a small dresser and tossing them onto the bed. One of them appeared to be a small phallus. And a few of the packets looked like condoms.

"What's going on?"

She tried to move, but her legs were weak. Desire was still pounding through her.

The woman came toward her again, the same dangerous look in her eyes.

She stood in front of Mary and unabashedly unzipped her leather vest. Pale, soft flesh began to appear followed by the slight bounce and emergence of full, round breasts.

Mary felt her mouth water as she focused on the smooth, tan areolas hardening in front of her. They continued to bunch as the woman moved closer, and Mary saw that the nipples were thick and firm and had a pink hue to them. The colliding colors made her think of strength and femininity mixed together as one.

The woman's gaze swept over Mary's face and Mary knew the hunger and excitement she felt could be seen through the heat of her skin and the pulse she felt careening in her neck.

"You want to stay?" the woman asked, her voice strong and serious.

Mary forced a "yes."

"If you say yes again then you will mean it. If you want me to stop you must say stop. No other word will do. Do you understand this, Mary?"

"Yes."

"Do you want to stay?"

This was her chance to run. But even if she had wanted to, she wouldn't have been able. Her body was melting, her mind rapid-firing with yes yes yes. All that mattered was her. This woman. This Goddamned gorgeous woman.

She stared into the mysterious eyes and nodded. "Yes."

"Then you only touch me where and when I tell you." Right away, the woman took Mary's hands and tugged them up to her breasts. She helped Mary massage them as she slinked up next to her.

"Feel, Mary," she purred.

Fire burned beneath Mary's skin. "I am." The breasts were warm and buoyant and she was stirred and shy all at once.

"Like this." The woman took Mary's fingers and pinched the nipples. "Do it," she said.

Mary began to stutter with nerves but the woman insisted. "Do it. Do it hard."

Mary pinched the firm knob and the woman hissed with pleasure. Her reaction sent a wave of pressure to Mary's center, making her flesh throb.

"Do both," the woman demanded. "Now."

Mary did and the woman laughed wickedly and shoved into her, biting her neck. "Yes, Mary. Like that. Harder." The woman nibbled and laughed in her ear. "Do you know what you are doing to me?" She pulled away and stilled Mary's hands. "Do you?"

"No." Mary's voice sounded meek.

The woman unfastened her leather pants while holding Mary's gaze. Then with Mary's hand in hers, she shoved it down the front to the waiting flesh between her legs.

At once Mary felt the slick folds, as hot and slippery as liquid sun. The woman shivered with pleasure, an intent grin on her face.

She pressed hard into Mary's sternum, shoving her against the wall. A small noise of surprise escaped Mary just as the woman's mouth attacked hers. The kiss was forceful, powerful, and all-consuming. Moans came from the woman as she conquered with her long, agile tongue. Mary felt her tremble, felt her slick flesh throb beneath her fingers.

The kiss deepened, the woman nearly eating her alive. When she pulled away, Mary saw the red blooming on her beautiful cheekbones, giving color to her soft grunts and rapid breathing.

Her golden eyes were slitted with need and her lips kept turning up at the corners, the pleasure obviously hard to control. When it seemed to become too much, or maybe not enough, she wrapped strong fingers around Mary's wrist and clenched her teeth, showing Mary the motion she wanted.

The woman grunted again and her eyes went wide with lust and need and hunger. Veins stood out in her neck, and Mary felt the woman's flesh flood and engorge. She rocked her hips, banging into Mary's hand. She appeared serious and fierce, and Mary knew at once she'd never seen anything so incredible. Her own groan of pleasure escaped her lips as she pleased her, and just as the woman was about to go insane, she jerked Mary's hand from her pants, shoved her full on against the wall, and then tore open her blouse.

Mary tried to speak, completely unsure of what to say, but the woman silenced her with a flash of her hungry eyes and the fastening of her mouth to Mary's aching breasts, biting and sucking through her bra.

The sensation was overwhelming one second and not nearly enough the next. Mary wanted to call out for more, hold the woman's head to her, and *demand* more. God, she just *needed* more. But before she could do anything, strong hands tore the blouse from her arms and then tugged at the bra straps, pulling them from her shoulders. Mary clung desperately to the woman's head, and she called out with a strangled cry when the woman exposed her nipples and took them into her hot mouth.

Oh Jesus, oh God. It was so incredibly good. She arched her back, shoving more of herself into the woman's mouth. She went up on her tiptoes again, her head tilting back against the wall. The mouth worked her, somehow touching every sensitive spot on her body just by sucking and licking and enveloping her nipple. And it started all over again when the woman left her and fastened on to her other one.

Intense waves of pleasure began to pass through her. Her clitoris ached, throbbing along with the waves, riding them into shore again and again. The woman bit her, holding her stiff nipple between her teeth. More deep laughter came just before she released her, her teeth tugging on her in a playful manner.

Mary swallowed with difficulty and nearly sank to the carpet once more. Her bones were soft and bowing and she could feel her arousal beginning to pool between her legs. Standing was nearly impossible; she was overwhelmed with pleasure and desire. If it hadn't been so damn good, it would've surely terrified her.

Knowing hands chased the thought away as they pulled her into the woman's arms. Mary was lost in her eyes for the briefest of seconds before being lifted and placed carefully onto the bed. She watched in a blissfully helpless manner as the woman removed her shoes, slacks, and then panties. The woman's eyes were still burning with that dangerous look, and they seemed to eat Mary alive as they traveled over her nude body. Mary knew she should feel self-conscious, but under the heat of her hungry stare she felt…wanted.

The woman met her gaze, and her muscles stiffened beneath her tanned skin as if an incredibly powerful thought had just raced through her. She swallowed and her eyes glinted. With what Mary couldn't tell. Suddenly, the woman moved and worked hurriedly, slipping into a harness that hugged her ass and pelvic area. Then she attached the phallus and bit into a wrapped condom, tearing off the cover. Mary stared as she slid the condom onto the phallus, rolling it downward with agile fingertips. Then she opened a small bottle and stroked on some clear lubricant.

Mary's heart rate kicked up once again as she studied the woman. She was lost in the way the woman's tendons and muscles moved, the slight sway of her pale breasts, the fisted stroking of her strong hand moving up and down over the phallus.

Mary scooted backward on the bed, wanting to be under the covers, wanting to watch the woman for hours from the head of the bed as she did things unimaginable to her. Mary shivered, turned on and confused. The thoughts were firing from a place inside she never knew existed. A frightening place. An exciting place. A demanding place.

The woman watched as Mary scrambled beneath the covers. Then she crawled toward her, breasts and phallus bobbing. She moved like a lioness on the hunt. She pulled the covers back and slid in next to Mary, her lips a centimeter from her ear.

"Open your legs, Mary." And her hand followed her command, lightly stroking up Mary's inner thigh. Delicate fingertips worked her, awakening her skin, first on one thigh, then the other.

Mary inhaled sharply and buried her face in the woman's neck as the woman nibbled and kissed along her ear and jawline.

"That is it, Mary. Feel me." Her hand moved higher and Mary's legs fell open, eager for her touch. "Yes, Mary."

The nimble fingers teased, brushing through Mary's fine hairs. Mary sighed at the sensation and nearly burst out of her skin when the woman took her nipple in her mouth just as expert fingers found her painfully engorged clitoris.

"Ah!" Mary clung to her as the fingers and tongue moved in sync with each other. Around and around they both went, driving her mad. Mary gyrated her hips, the sensation so incredibly good. She relaxed her legs further with her knees flat on the bed, opening up fully, offering her wet, hungry flesh. The woman moved lower, hissing a long "yes" as she tunneled under the covers, trailing her hot mouth down Mary's abdomen to her inner thighs to where her hand had been expertly playing.

"Watch, Mary," she said as she threw back the covers and settled between her legs. Mary lifted her head and struggled to breathe as the woman began sucking on her inner thighs and working her tongue upward and into Mary's folds. When it hit her virgin flesh, she cried out and gripped her head. The woman continued, finding her clit right away, flicking it mercilessly, opening Mary further with the outward press of her thumbs.

"Oh, Jesus." The muffled throb of the club had settled inside her once again, now beating beneath her clit as the woman teased it and plied it with attention from her heavy, slick tongue. Faster and harder. Faster and harder. Until Mary was lifting her hips from the bed, giving herself to her, pleasure shooting through her like liquid fire. Seeing the woman there, feeling her, fucking needing her there, it was driving her crazy, shoving her, slapping her, shaking her. Awakening her from that deep, dark, lonely and senseless place she'd been hiding away in for years. She was breaking out now, stepping into the light, screaming at the sun.

She tightened her fingers in the woman's hair wanting her to remain at that spot, doing that motion for all eternity. Yes, yes, just like that. She began to say it, mumbling it at first but then insisting and demanding. It only seemed to fuel the woman more, causing her to groan and take her clit into her lips where she held it captive, teasing. Mary begged.

"Don't stop. God. Please."

She called out in surprise when the woman released her and moved lower, snaking her tongue around her opening. Mary lifted herself trying to see, her flesh demanding it of her. It was its own entity now and it needed to be pleased. She could feel herself trying to wrap around the woman's face.

"You are so wet, Mary. So, so wet."

Mary knew she was, could feel it ebbing out of her and into the woman's face and mouth. The woman was consuming her. Literally. Oh, what a fucking insanely sexy realization. There was no possible way it could get any better. No possible way—oh Jesus God, the woman's tongue was inside her, thrusting up into her.

Mary whimpered and clutched the bed covers. The thumping of the club grew deeper, shaking the wall. It could've come down around her and she wouldn't have cared. Nothing could've torn her away from the woman and her all-knowing, all-seeking tongue. Mary clenched her eyes closed and rocked her hips. She needed more. More more more.

And then there was nothing. No tongue, no lips, no hot breath bearing down on her. Her eyes flew open only to see the woman come forward, settling between Mary's hips.

"It is time," the woman said, bracing herself above Mary with one arm while the other moved down to the phallus. Mary felt her move it, felt it all cold and slick and waiting entry at her opening. Her heart went off like a string of firecrackers as she realized what was about to happen.

"Look at me, Mary. Look into my eyes."

They were burning still, like a predator willing to take its prey in the most humane way possible. And then she pressed into her and Mary at once felt the hot glide of the phallus. It filled her completely and took her breath away. It tightened her throat and curled her toes. She couldn't speak, could barely take enough breath to stave off passing out. And then it was in further and she dug her nails into the woman's back, crying out in short gasps as the woman kissed her neck and thrust slowly.

Another thrust came and the woman kissed her, dominating her with her tongue and powerful lips. She kissed her again and again, tongue swirling as her hips moved, picking up the pace. Mary clung to her, bit into her neck, making her groan. The thrusting increased, and Mary called out, the burning fading into the sweetest of ecstasy.

This was what the licking had prepared her for. This was the final act. The big show.

"God," she let out, her head arching back into the pillow. It was good, it was thrilling, and it was coming with every pound and shake of the walls. The woman was fucking her, filling her with pleasure, and it was hot and passionate and sexy, powerful in ways she never could've imagined.

She licked the woman's neck and tasted her moist skin. She kissed her, this time using her tongue to swirl in her mouth. She grabbed her leather covered ass and forced herself up against her.

"Fucking good," she managed to say. "Oh God, fuck me so good."

The woman made a noise of excited approval and she pinned Mary's wrists above her head. Her head bent to attack Mary's breasts as she continued to sway into her, sending Mary into a tailspin of ecstasy.

"I—yes. Oh fuck, yes."

The woman bit her, tugged firmly on her nipple. Then she propped herself up and fucked her harder. Faster. Just like her tongue had done. Harder and faster. Harder and faster. Mary gripped her neck and stared into her. Every muscle in her own body felt tense and full, absorbing the heavy pleasure. She held her breath and took, took, took. She pulled herself up, made grunting noises, and the woman pummeled pleasure between her legs.

"Oh God." And then she shot back onto the bed and her body went into pleasure-soaked spasms. Her head shook from side to side, her pelvis moved on its own accord, and white-hot floaters filled her vision. She couldn't get enough. Never would be able to get enough. She clung to the woman's back, swearing she'd never let go. She tried to tell her all this, but nothing would come. Her voice box had caved in and blown away with the orgasm like dead leaves on a windy day. Still, she tried, holding again to her neck, tangling her fingers in her hair. She managed to groan, to eke out her pleasure on strangled bits of breath.

The woman kissed her. So long and warm and sweet tasting. When she pulled away she had that mysterious look to her that she'd had just before she crawled onto the bed. Mary watched her and knew she'd never be able to get her face from her mind ever again.

CHAPTER THREE

Mary. Sweet Mary. Jude had never had anyone so sweet and so pure, so damned ripe and responsive.

She could feel her moving beneath her, her throbbing flesh already wanting more. She was insatiable, absolutely insatiable.

There would never be another like her. Jude knew this, and as disappointing as the realization was, it also lit a fire beneath every fiber of her being. She had to make it last, had to take her time and relish this.

She moaned into her mouth, pulled away, and gently slid out of her. Breathless, she ran her hands over Mary's hips and thighs, as if she were creating something special inside her. She tried to burn Mary's image and the way she felt beneath her mouth and fingertips into her mind. But like a dream she couldn't quite grasp or return to, she couldn't totally capture her. Mary was too good to ever completely and fully re-experience through memory alone.

"Turn over," Jude said after staring at her for a long minute. She lifted Mary's hip and encouraged her to roll. When Mary did, she eased her hips up and began running her tongue up her thighs to the smooth cheeks of her ass where she bit and sucked. Mary held herself up on all fours, flinching in ecstasy at every touch.

Loving her reactions, Jude moved along her back, breathing on her skin, licking her all the way down to her opening. Once there, she teased with her tongue, enjoying the cool slickness of Mary's desire. She moved lower and flicked her swollen clit. Mary jerked and stilled and then pressed back more, arching herself. Her cries were soft and muffled, as if she didn't want Jude to know just how good it felt. As if she were afraid she would stop or take the pleasure away. At that moment, Jude knew she could give to Mary all night long and it wouldn't be enough. Not for Mary and not for her. While there was danger in that, she couldn't bring herself to stop or slow. Instead, she kept flicking her clit, loving the feel of it and the way Mary was starting to rock back into her mouth.

When it became too much, she gripped her legs and inched up to tongue fuck her. Mary pleaded, crying for more. Jude knew the sensation wasn't nearly enough, but she was thoroughly enjoying teasing her and she loved the way her wet walls were warm and soft and throbbing for more. She could've eaten her all night, saturating her hole and flicking her clit, taking it in to suck on every once in a while. Until Mary was howling and dripping and ferocious in her need to come. But her own impatience got the better of her, and her desire to please Mary caused her to straighten and ease the shaft of the cock into her opening. Mary cried out, and when it sank into her further, her voice fell away.

"Do you like it?" Jude asked. She had to hear Mary's wavering voice, had to know what her cock felt like as she thrust into her, gripping her hips as she moved.

Mary shoved backward, the pleasure obvious and already mounting. "Ye-es."

Jude watched as Mary pushed into the sheets with tightly bent fingers. She watched as she lowered her chest, thrusting her ass further into the air.

She pumped her harder, quicker. The phallus made a sucking noise as it fucked her. Jude closed her eyes, overcome with a rush of heat to her own flesh as Mary continued to groan.

"Ye-es, ye-es, ye-es," Mary said continuously.

Jude kept pumping, the imagined sensation of the fucking cock so real and so sweet she could almost feel it herself. But they both needed more. She opened her eyes and focused with intent. She reached around Mary to frame her clit with her fingers and they both called out in ecstasy with Mary forcing her chest up, rocking back with her ass.

"Don't stop. Don't stop," Mary commanded as her hands tangled in the sheets and she pushed back further.

Jude grabbed her hips and shoved harder, full on fucking her. There was no careful gentleness now. No sweet, soft, phallic thrusting. This was fucking. Hard and fast and unapologetic, her body completely taking over as if the cock had invaded her consciousness. She was insane with pumping and Mary loved it, couldn't get enough.

"More, more, more," she cried until she screamed in beautiful throat-collapsing bliss, again and again, coming once more, this time so loudly the music seemed to challenge her rather than drown her out. She reared back, pushing herself up to her knees, grinding herself onto the phallus with the forced gyration of her hips, her hand holding fiercely to the fingers framing her clit.

Completely overcome and moved by the spectacle, Jude took Mary's earlobe in her mouth and whispered to her. "So beautiful, Mary. So sexy."

Mary cried out some more, quaked for several long seconds, and then collapsed onto the bed and languished there on her back.

Jude watched her breathe for a few moments, taking in the way Mary's beautiful flesh contrasted slightly with the sheets. She studied her passion-painted mouth, her cheekbones, the light blue veins running blood through her delicate hands and neck. Several more seconds passed as she stared down at her. She was so completely moved and turned on she hesitated to speak. She'd never been too moved to speak before.

Mary.

Why was she affecting her so?

Mary rolled over and blinked her large, freshly moist eyes at Jude. She had the look of a woman loved, heat coloring her cheeks, faint marks of teeth, tongue, and hunger on her neck and chest. And those eyes. They were now eyes that had seen but wanted to see so much more, despite the obvious hint of danger the club gave off.

"Who are you?" Mary asked, surprising her. Her voice was back, though not as strong as it once had been. "Tell me your name."

Jude still didn't trust herself to speak.

"Please."

Finally, after looking deeply into her eyes, Jude said all that she could say. "Come here."

She tugged Mary forward by her legs and rested them on her shoulders, with the phallus once again at Mary's opening.

As she entered her, Mary arched her back and clung once again to the bedsheets.

A word came to her then. The one on her lips all along. She said it over and over as she fucked her.

"Mary."

CHAPTER FOUR

S hh. Here she comes. Here she comes."

Mary eyed her whispering co-workers just before removing her shoulder bag and dropping heavily into her chair. The huddled mass of gossips were then out of sight, hidden beyond the walls of her small cubicle. Normally, she'd cringe knowing they were talking about her, but this morning she was too exhausted to care.

In fact, she was amazed she was at work and sitting upright in front of her computer. How had she gotten there? She touched her temple and barely recalled how she'd come out of her stupor on the couch, stumbled into clothes, and driven on autopilot all the way to the office.

She stared at her desk and fought to keep her eyes focused. The office smelled of freshly brewed coffee and warm popcorn. Both seemed to be making her nauseous. In the near distance she heard soft laughter. Her co-workers were no doubt still discussing her, wondering if she'd gone to meet them the night before.

At Conquest.

If only they knew. If only *she* knew. She still couldn't quite accept all that had happened as actual reality. Had she really gone there and slept with a perfect stranger? A fiercely sexy, foreign stranger? Yes. She had. Her sore and tingling body told her so. And her mind, which had yet to fully awaken, was already replaying image after clit-throbbing image. Oh God, it had been good. More than just good. It had been intense and passionate and soul stirring.

She pressed her legs together as a rush of excitement raced to her flesh.

The woman. Who was she? What was her name?

Mary could recall every word, foreign or not. Every touch, every kiss, every lick.

Her computer came to life as she scooted forward and took control of the mouse. She went to a site for free language translations and tried to type in the words the woman had kept saying to her. But she had no idea how to spell them.

Sighing, she went from that site to a German dictionary where she scrolled down to a word she recognized as one used by the woman repeatedly. It meant beautiful.

Her breath paused in her chest. Beautiful. Oh God, the woman was amazing and she thought Mary was beautiful. She had to see her again.

Mary began searching for Conquest. She had to find her. No one had ever touched her like that, stirred her like that. Ever. And certainly no one had fucked her. And if they had, it would've never been like that. So long and so good she'd had to be helped from the club when it was over, her legs wobbly and weak like a spent rubber band.

Mary'd tried like hell to get her name, to please her in return, just as she'd been pleased. But the woman had only pushed her hands away and ignored her questions, giving away nothing but sweet, dripping pleasure.

The computer didn't help much either, only giving the name and location of the club. Mary continued to search, desperate for information despite the possibility of getting in trouble for searching such content on the office computer. To her bewilderment, she realized that she wasn't afraid. Was she? She knew others did it, but still. No, she wasn't afraid. Let them say something. She would hopefully have her information, and that was all that mattered. The rest could go to hell. Including her co-workers.

The new attitude felt good. She wondered how long it would last.

"I have to see her," she said softly, already working out ways to do so. She would call the club. And ask for…who?

Shit.

"Mary, hi."

Mary turned and found Carla Meeker leaning on the cubicle, smiling down at her.

"Hello." Mary's tone was one of boredom and disinterest. She was in no mood for small talk. It wasn't new for her, but this time the reason behind it was different. She didn't just simply want to avoid a conversation because she was shy and had nothing to say. This time she just didn't want to look at Meeker's face and listen to her bullshit.

"I just stopped by to see how your night went."

Mary fought hardening her eyes. The gall. What a bitch, coming over there and actually asking about her night. Mary clicked her mouse and refocused on the computer. She'd minimized the screen with her sex club search on it, and now she was pretending like she was working. Maybe Meeker would get the hint.

"I wanted to apologize for not getting a chance to buy you that drink. Rain check?"

The way she said rain check made Mary's skin crawl. It was so high-pitched it felt like she'd just run her nails across a chalkboard.

Mary stopped typing and looked up at her. Meeker was a woman's woman, all style and pretty poise and gossip. Perfect hairdo, perfect makeup, perfect nails. She always seemed to say the perfect thing at the perfect time. And her clothes were to die for, according to the others. But Mary wasn't in to the whole girly, ruffly thing.

"What do you say?" Meeker asked with a zillion watt smile, her voice climbing again.

Mary didn't even bother putting up a fight or laying into her for setting her up. She had other things to attend to and way more important things on her mind. Like that gorgeous, ripped, incredibly talented blonde for starters. So instead Mary decided to fuck with her. Shrugging, she said, "Sure."

Meeker seemed surprised, and Mary caught her glancing over the cubicle, probably looking toward the others for guidance. They obviously wanted to know if she'd showed last night. But she wasn't going to give them the satisfaction of knowing.

"Uh, okay."

"Yeah, that sounds good," Mary said, once again focusing on her computer. "You let me know when and where."

Meeker seemed to fight for words, and Mary couldn't help but gloat at the sight. It was like watching a flopping fish struggle to breathe on a boat deck, the seconds ticking by painfully slowly, the fish finally lying still, gills yawning, desperate for water. Mary would gladly relieve the fish with water, but for Meeker, no way.

"Okay," she finally said.

Mary didn't miss a beat. "Okay then. See you later."

Meeker walked away and Mary heard the others pounce on her with hurried questions. The fuckers. Ugh, God, why hadn't she stayed home? She didn't need this crap today. She dropped her head into her hands, wishing she could go home and curl up to dream about her encounter with the woman. But she wouldn't be able to sleep or rest, much less sit still enough to dream.

Standing, Mary searched for her colleagues just over the cubicle wall. To her relief, they had dispersed. As she returned to her seat she retrieved the business card with Conquest on it. Taking a deep breath, she grabbed the phone and dialed information. She gave the name and the address and, to her surprise, there was a listing. Her heart pounded as the line rang. Her heart rate slowed, though, as the ringing continued. Eventually, it connected to a nondescript voice mail. She cleared her throat and spoke, trying not to be too loud.

"Uh, hello. My name is Mary. Mary Brunelle. I was there last night and spent some time with a tall blond woman. She was German I believe. Anyway, I was hoping to get a hold of her. Can you please have her call me?" She rattled off her cell number and hung up quickly. She was hunched over her phone like a secret cannibal devouring someone's ribs. If anyone had happened to pass by, they would know immediately she was guilty of something.

Forcing out a breath, she eased back against her chair and waited. Oh, no. What if they just used caller ID and called the office instead of her cell? Shit. Quickly, she redialed the number and left another voice mail, this time emphasizing that her cell only should be called and preferably before five because she had a class some nights. But any time after seven would be fine.

She hung up and at once felt utterly ridiculous. A class? As if that were more important than the woman? She must've sounded like a child. She stared at her cell phone, willing it to ring. But it didn't. She stared some more. Willed some more. But nothing.

When her boss walked by, she appeared busy. When co-workers wandered by, she did the same. And when the office phone finally rang, she nearly jumped out of her skin. She answered with all stutters and nerves. But it was strictly business and not anyone from Conquest.

By the time four thirty came around, she was so wound up she felt like she needed a stiff drink. She'd checked and rechecked her voice mail on her cell phone, triple checking that she hadn't somehow missed a phone call. There were no messages, though. No missed phone calls. For whatever reason, the woman hadn't called.

She pondered this as she gathered her things and left the office. Why hadn't she called? Did she not get the message? Maybe no one was at Conquest until evening. That was possible. She tried to relax a little, allowing that excuse to swim around in her brain for a while. If worse came to worst, she could always just go back over there.

Could I?

What about tonight?

No, not tonight. Give her a chance to call first.

She wound her way through the parking lot and found her car. She had just pressed the button on her keyless remote when she heard some snickers coming from nearby. Three of her co-workers were leaning against a car, cigarettes in hand, smirks on their faces.

"Hey, Mary, how's it going?"

She wanted to just lower her head and get inside the car like she usually did. She hated these guys, these three assholes in particular. Her instincts told her they were probably the ones behind the joke even though they hadn't been included in the original deal to meet her there. She wouldn't have gone if they had been.

"Where are you off to in such a hurry?"

She tossed her shoulder bag onto the passenger seat and straightened, staring into the evening sun.

"Home." She straightened her clothes just like she often did when nervous.

"Home? That's what you say every night, Mary. Don't you have a life?" They laughed softly as the leader, Wade, sucked hard on his cigarette, as if amused by himself. She watched his cheeks cave in and she wished like hell his whole face would follow, sucked into some nameless void to be gone forever.

"I have a perfectly nice life," she said, her anxiety causing her words to sound hollow and weak.

"I bet you do," Wade said, elbowing the asshole next to him. He pushed himself away from the car and came toward her. "I bet you got a real nice life. See, everyone else thinks you don't. They think you're boring and uptight. A real meek little bitch."

The words stung as if she'd been slapped. Still, she tried to hide it by squaring her shoulders and clenching her jaw. She hoped he didn't notice her trembling.

Tears fought to surface.

She hated this about herself. No matter how strong and confident she felt inside, her body always snapped and rattled like a weak twig in the wind.

Wade seemed to eat it up as he drew closer. "But I disagree. I stick up for you, Mary. Because I know you. I know that beneath that uptight little exterior lies a lioness. A real sex kitten."

Laughter erupted and Wade cocked his head a little, as if waiting to see if she might be amused.

Mary shook with anger and embarrassment. She couldn't speak. Couldn't move. She just stood there and took it, trying her damndest not to cry.

Wade reached out and touched her face with rough feeling knuckles. The cigarette smoke burned her eyes. She flinched and drew back, and this time he laughed along with his buddies.

"Go on home, Mary. Before the big bad wolf gets you."

He turned and walked back to his friends who continued to laugh. As she climbed in her car and wiped her eyes she heard him say, "No way, man. She didn't go. I'd bet my life on that."

She wished he really had bet his life on it, and she thought about that the entire drive home, crying and shaking and yelling at herself. Why couldn't she stand up for herself? Why did her voice always falter, caving in to tears and other emotion?

She had no answers, and when she got home, she changed her clothes and busied herself cleaning. She was wound up and angry, mostly at herself for taking Wade's shit. She should've slapped him. Or grinned back at him and given him a smart response. She should've done something, anything. But all she'd done was stand there like an idiot.

After cleaning the kitchen counters and dusting and vacuuming, she settled down on the couch and stared at her phone. There had been no calls. The television offered no answers and no entertainment. The woman still saturated her mind, bleeding through Wade and his bullying, saturating him completely to where he was helpless and unable to harm her in her mind. She imagined the woman confronting him, giving him a powerful punch and a good talking to. Then she imagined her wrapping her arm around her protectively before leading her away to safety.

The woman could handle Wade. Probably put him to his knees. She'd love to see that.

Mary picked up her phone and took a deep breath as she redialed the club. This time someone answered, a gruff sounding man, and she almost hung up.

"Yeah? Hello?"

She closed her eyes and forced herself to speak. "Yes, hi. I called earlier and left a message. My name is Mary. I'm looking for the woman I, uh, met with last night. She's taller and blond and—"

"Yeah, yeah hang on a sec."

Her heart thundered. There was muffled movement and she could hear his voice but couldn't make out what he was saying. Her heart stilled and fell when it was him who came back on.

"Yeah, Mary is it?"

"Yes."

"She ain't here."

"Oh. Well, when will she be there?"

"She doesn't keep a schedule, sweetheart. This ain't a doctor's office. We don't take appointments."

"Oh." She felt foolish but still at a loss. "Is there any way she could call me back?"

"I'll give her the message. But I wouldn't hold my breath."

There was a click and a sharp dial tone.

It seemed to exemplify her day. Sighing, she sunk further into the couch and closed her eyes.

Chapter Five

Jude entered the club by the back door and strode purposely to her room. The heavy throb of the music and the electricity from the pleasure seeking patrons felt charged and thick as she wove between sweaty bodies.

Some reached out for her and spoke, turned on and surprised at her civilian attire. But their hungry fingers and hungry come-ons fell short of truly touching her, just like they always did.

She recognized a few of those hungry faces, but she had no interest, knowing a sensitive little fuck here and there wouldn't do. No, not tonight.

Even the ones that dressed the part and talked the talk and thought they wanted a real, true fuck couldn't handle her at full force. And she was in no mood to cater to their sudden tender needs or "my husband doesn't want me" tears.

She strode confidently, ignoring them all as she headed for her room. Once inside, she closed the door, locked it, and then stripped out of her clothes. What she needed tonight wasn't lingering in the hallway, batting long lashes or pushing out amped up breasts in new leather vests. As she opened her duffel bag and stepped into her leather garb, she tried to imagine what exactly it was she did need. She couldn't quite put her finger on it, but she knew the second she saw it, she'd know.

Her imagination soared as she continued to get ready, doing her hair and spraying on cologne. The woman she needed would be consumed in a halo of light as she entered the club, a dangerous look in her eye and a purpose in her step. She'd push all others aside with her brazen confidence and walk right up to Jude, daring her.

Jude would take that dare, slam her against the wall, and conquer her right there in front of the others. She'd bite into her neck and—a familiar cry of firstborn lust echoed through her head. She tried to shake it away, but it kept coming, this time along with the pale, smooth, giving flesh beneath her hungry teeth.

It was Mary's cry.

Mary's flesh.

Mary.

Mary had taken her full on and had begged for more. She'd come for her again and again.

And Jude had let her touch her, taking her hands within the first few minutes and insisting on it. Jude had never wanted anyone's touch before, not at Conquest, and she'd never allowed it. But Mary was different. She'd *wanted* her touch.

She steadied herself against the dresser as she remembered how she'd almost come in her hand. Sweet, innocent Mary had stroked her aching flesh and stared into her face like she was God. And it had almost shattered her to pieces. It was why she'd made her stop.

It had taken years to pick those pieces up, and it no doubt would again, no matter how beautiful and pleasurable the pieces were, even if they were brought about by Mary. She couldn't risk that loss of control again. She couldn't allow someone else to slip inside her chest and command the beating and feeling of her heart. It had hurt too much before and the puppeteer of her heart had turned on her, slashing and squeezing her heart, leaving it murdered and useless, a dead lump inside her. Just thinking about it again caused a cold sweat to break out over her. She had to remind herself that she was okay now, her heart fine and though scarred, recovered and functioning. Her one and only relationship was long past and she pushed it from her mind, refusing to think of her ex. That refusal was how she'd survived and that wasn't about to change now.

A series of loud knocks came from the door, tearing her from her thoughts. She was grateful for the distraction. Her leather vest and pants felt cool and snug against her skin as she moved and when she opened the door she saw Cord standing there looking at her in his boorish manner, fists at his side, moisture crowning his brow. His coarse chest hair fought against the leather pressing into his broad but somewhat flabby pectorals. Vodka and sweat permeated around him.

They rarely spoke and when they did it wasn't without important purpose. He thrust his hand forward and she caught sight of a piece of paper wadded up in his palm. She took it and opened it, knowing at once what it was. Cord, too, acted as if it were old news.

"She's called a few times. Left messages. Sorta hyper."

"Thanks."

"Yeah."

He left her there alone in her room, blue and red bulbs bleeding. She closed the door and sat on her bed. The paper read, *Mary Brunelle from last night. Wants you to call her,* in Cord's barely legible handwriting. A phone number was scribbled below it. She ran her thumbs over it recalling Mary and everything that had come with her. The innocence, the sincerity, the trepidation. Her moans, her cries, and her orgasmic pleas. She would love to have her again. The mere thought alone slammed her blood through her body in a maddening pace, even more so than her fantasy only moments before. The reaction wasn't welcomed, and she didn't allow it to continue for more than a few seconds. She'd been battling it all day long and had hardly slept when she'd finally arrived home the night before.

Rising, she crumpled the paper and tossed it in the corner bin. She'd tell Cord to ignore any messages from her, just as she did all the others.

This was why she had rules.

Mary Brunelle was dangerous, intentionally so or not.

And from here on out, she was off limits.

Another knock sounded and relief pushed out with her breath as she opened the door. Finally. A distraction.

"Hi." The blonde was short and fit, still dressed in the suit she'd probably worn to work. Her perfume was strong, a lot like her attitude and eager confidence. There was no halo of light, but it wasn't needed. Jude saw all she needed to see in the determined, keen glimmer of her eyes.

"Come in." Jude moved aside and watched as the blonde strode past. She'd had her several times before, forcefully, holding her up against the wall, legs splayed, sharp high heels pointed outward while she called out to God, the large dildo forcing her in and pulling her out with its thick mass.

Oh fuck yes, she would do. She would *have* to do.

"Where do you want me?" she asked with a coy look on her well made up face.

Jude clenched her jaw and shoved Mary from her mind for the umpteenth time.

"Everywhere."

CHAPTER SIX

C lass. Mary wasn't looking forward to it.
It was round two of Spanish and something she had to take for work. The company was starting to advertise as bilingual, and it was either jump on board or jump ship. So she'd jumped on board hesitantly and was still clinging to her life vest. The good news was she was supposed to get a decent sized raise after completion of four classes, so she was keeping her eye on that, plus the fact that she'd hopefully be somewhat fluent in Spanish by the end of it all.

It really wasn't that awful and she'd actually enjoyed the first class and had learned quite a bit. She'd taken the first class online, only going to the campus to take her final exam. This round was an on-campus class, and she was more than a little nervous. But at the very least it got her out of work a little early. Anything was worth that. Even a nerve-racking hour and a half at the college four days a week.

She kept telling herself that as she walked to class. Numerous others passed her by, and she knew that normally she'd be staring at the ground, avoiding gazes and hellos. But all she could think about was class ending so she could swing by Conquest.

To her dismay, the woman from the club hadn't called. Mary had sat by the phone all night long, watching reruns well into morning. Finally, she'd drifted off to sleep only to dream about her. When she'd awakened, she was convinced they had met up again. Only after a long, hot shower did she realize it had only been a dream. Disappointment had weighed her down after that. She couldn't seem to shake it. Why hadn't she called? Mary had gone over it repeatedly in her mind. Surely she'd received the message by now. Surely.

And yet, no call.

By the time four thirty had rolled around she'd tossed her cell into her purse, refusing to keep staring at it. She'd have to take matters into her own hands and just drive back over to Conquest after class.

But what if the woman called while she was in class? She wouldn't be able to take the call.

The door banged shut behind her as she entered a large lecture hall. All heads turned to face her and she lowered her gaze, refusing to meet their stares as she wound her way to a seat in the middle. She settled in and willed the heat in her face to disperse as she dug out her cell phone and placed it on silent mode.

With her palms on the desktop, she forced herself to calm down and think of nothing but her encounter at Conquest. If the woman called while she was in class, she would quickly excuse herself and leave the room to answer. She was suddenly giddy at the thought of her calling. How quickly hope had come again and it left her feeling sure the woman would call. She would be done with her day job—surely she had a day job—and she would be heading to Conquest for another night of seduction. She'd get Mary's message and immediately call, having been just as moved by their encounter as Mary had been.

Yes, and then they'd meet and fall into each other's arms and make love for hours, declaring their need for each other the entire time. They'd confess they never could be apart and that they should live together in a cottage off the lake where they could lie together in front of the fire and make love out in the water under a moonlit sky.

As ridiculous as she knew it was, it didn't stop her from thoroughly enjoying the fantasy. She nearly sighed as she continued to dream, cheek resting in her hand. Her blissful thoughts were interrupted by a man walking in and placing a book bag on the front desk. He moved quickly, almost too quickly for his small stature. And when he spoke, the words tumbled out just as fast. Mary fished out a notebook and wrote down the info the man had written on the board. His name was something Mary couldn't even pronounce and this was his first class ever. A few of the students made snide comments, but the man wouldn't hear of it. He flashed a smile after he finished with the board and then got busy passing out the syllabus. Mary nearly groaned as she read it over and noted all the vocabulary quizzes. She did groan when she came across the oral participation and oral presentations.

She wondered if she could get out of it. Maybe take the course online again. Damn it, no. They didn't offer one. And the oral participation was probably why.

She had to find a way around it. It was making her throat tighten just imagining it. The vocabulary she could do. Answering a question or two in class she could manage to suffer through. But oral presentations? Oh Jesus—

She couldn't do this. She'd throw up the second she had to stand to speak. She had to talk to the teacher to find out if this was absolutely mandatory. She glanced at the front of the room, hoping to find him alone and easy to approach. But he wasn't alone, and her worried heart froze in her chest.

There was a woman. Standing there talking to her teacher. She looked like—was—oh God—she was tall and blond with a similar haircut, and when she turned—oh God, she had the same sharp cheekbones.

Mary gripped the top of her desk, desperate to hang on.

Her teacher stood smiling, nodding his head in a slow and maddening way. Mary couldn't take it. Her breathing grew quick and sharp, causing the woman next to her to turn and stare.

Mary was dizzy with blood-thrumming excitement, and her teacher finally introduced the woman. Professor something. Mary strained to hear. Goddamn it, speak up! He continued. She was a professor. Professor Jaeger. Head of the foreign language department. He wrote it on the board.

Oh God. Was this happening? Was it really her?

And then she spoke and Mary about fell from her chair as that thick German accent poured out in heavy power and grace. A whimper of sheer passionate recall escaped Mary, and she slapped her hand over her mouth, hoping no one had heard. But it was too late. The entire class was staring at her. Including Professor Jaeger.

Mary tried to look away, her embarrassment demanding it of her, but she couldn't tear her eyes from Professor Jaeger. And for a moment it seemed as though the professor couldn't look away either. Their eyes were locked, and for the briefest of seconds, just at the initial glance, Mary saw that she recognized her. Her chiseled face went slack and her cheeks tinged slightly. But a half second later she recovered with a stone-like look, taking in Mary just like the others, as if she were merely an observer, wondering what the crazy student in the center of the room was making a fuss about.

Slowly, the class began to look forward again, shaking Mary off like the kind of minor and brief nuisance a car alarm would draw. Her teacher did the same and so did Professor Jaeger, speaking as calmly as she had that night at Conquest, giving instruction and encouraging students to come see the faculty if they were in any way struggling.

Mary squirmed and thought about the kind of help she needed.

It brought that hot pressure between her legs. It was a feeling she'd felt for the first time at Conquest, and she knew she'd feel it frequently from here on out. The path had been cleared for it and another rush of it came as she continued to watch Professor Jaeger.

She had on black slacks, black dress shoes, and a tight-fitting pale blouse. Her hair was worn down and over in the front, giving her a softer, more professional look. Small hoop earrings framed her face. She looked good, classy. And still incredibly sexy.

Mary sat there eating Professor Jaeger alive with her eyes as if no one else in the room existed. She almost growled like a hungry dog possessively fastened to a bone. She dared anyone around her to rattle her or to speak to the professor. She'd pounce for sure.

Professor Jaeger. Jaeger. Mary said it over and over again in her mind. She liked the way it flowed, the way it seemed to have a taste to it. She imagined saying it just before taking her into her mouth.

Movement broke her thoughts. Professor Jaeger took a seat near the front desk, crossing her long legs to observe as Mary's teacher began class.

Mary tried to pay attention, but it was impossible. She could only stare at the back of Professor Jaeger's head and wait. Time ticked by slowly, painfully. Each second hurt, stabbing anticipation into her gut just like the clicking of a climbing rollercoaster.

Professor Jaeger was motionless, watching their teacher as he went over the synopsis and the first few pages of the textbook. She didn't seem fazed, didn't move an inch. How could she be so still? How could she not turn to glance at Mary knowing she was there?

Mary willed the clock onward, but inside she was in turmoil over what she would say when the chance arrived.

Words played through her mind. "Hi? Hello? Remember me? Because I sure as hell remember you. Take me home. Make me yours. I am yours. Completely. Oh God, just touch me again."

She nearly cried out again as if she'd spoken the words aloud. But more shocking was their meaning and truth, and she worried they would shock Professor Jaeger too.

She sounded crazy and over the top, but she couldn't help herself. It was like her mind and body were suddenly controlled by someone else. Or something else.

The word lust came to mind as she doodled in her notebook, making the same pressured marks again and again. Time ticked on and she refused to watch the clock. When she did finally look up again, Professor Jaeger was gone. Panicked, Mary stood and searched desperately. She had to be there. Somewhere. The corners. Behind the board. By the door. But she was nowhere to be seen.

The class was repeating vocabulary words in a muted drone, sounding like an old Spanish speaking machine. The professor seemed to have vanished in the drone.

Those around Mary once again craned their heads to stare at her. The teacher, too, stopped speaking and looked at her questioningly.

"Is there a problem?"

Mary felt her blood drop to her feet. "No." The digital clock showed ten minutes to go. She couldn't wait that long. She had to find her. "I mean yes. I need to be excused. Please."

The teacher lowered the book in his hands and gave a quiet, somewhat stunned nod. Mary hurried to gather her things. She left the class as they began to drone again, one Spanish noun after another.

In the hallway she froze, unsure which way to go. She still didn't know what she was going to say, but it didn't seem to matter because her body just kept moving, regardless.

This was all new turf to her. These weren't the unsure and uneasy feelings about the near future; those were old news. But this unshakable drive was new. This need and urge and ability to push on when the outcome was completely unpredictable. This was definitely new, and she seemed unable and unwilling to stop it. She hurried to her right and nearly sprinted as she searched. A few people were mingling here and there, but there was no sign of Professor Jaeger.

She headed out of the building and into the setting sun. Her breath came in short bursts as she thought. Where could she be? Maybe she'd already left. No. Mary wouldn't let herself think that way yet. She had to keep looking. The sun glinted off the sign of the next building. It held the faculty offices. With a big inhale, she marched up to the door and entered.

The building was quiet. All she could hear was the gentle circulation of air, like the sound of a silent airplane cabin in mid flight. She grew more nervous, as if everyone in their office had heard her enter. To her relief, no one appeared and she hurried to the directory where she quickly scanned for her name. She found it at once.

Professor Jude Jaeger. Director of Foreign Language.

Jude. Mary ran her fingertip over the name as her mind played with it. So strong and sexy. She imagined calling it out in the darkest of nights.

Mary lowered her hand and headed toward the proper wing. She was nervous, yes. Now more than ever. But she was more nervous about finding Jude already gone. She'd just found her treasure and to think it might have re-buried itself in an unknown and unmapped land nearly panicked her.

She quickened her step and counted off door number after door number. The closer she got, the more her adrenaline surged, until eventually she was heated and sweating and standing dead center in front of the correct doorway.

Jude was behind her desk, a Styrofoam cup of contents unknown paused mid movement in her hand. She stared at Mary but made no motion to move or react.

"Hi." The word came out on a shaky exhale and Mary stumbled over her feet as she came to the doorway. The word ridiculous came to mind as she forced a smile and tried to act suave. She ran a hand through her hair and eased a jittery hand in her pocket. "I'm glad I found you."

Jude took a sip from the cup and set it down. Her eyes had drifted down to her desktop where she began shuffling papers.

"How can I help you?" She didn't look up.

Mary fought chewing on her bottom lip. She was stumped. "I don't need any help. I mean, not like you mean. Don't you remember me?"

"From?"

Was she really doing this? Acting like they'd never met?

Mary took another step. "From Conquest. From the other night. We—"

Jude rose and hurriedly stalked toward her. Mary held her breath as she drew close then leaned over her to push the door closed.

"I'm sorry, I didn't mean to say it so loud. I just thought—"

"You just thought what?" Jude was holding the doorknob, her face etched in stone.

Mary found herself blinking. "I don't know."

"You don't know."

"No, I mean yes. I tried to call you. Left you messages. Why didn't you call me?"

Jude laughed and Mary felt foolish and frustrated. What the hell was so funny?

"What makes you sure I even got the message?" She released the doorknob and rounded Mary to lean back against the door, arms crossed over her chest. As sexy and domineering as she still was, Mary noticed that she looked tired.

"Because I left a lot of messages and one of them was with a man who said he'd give it to you. I just wanted to talk."

"Why?"

Mary searched for words. Jude was quicker.

"I don't talk, Mary."

"You do remember me." Her chest swelled and tiny little butterflies batted around her heart at hearing her name.

Jude's face clouded. "I don't talk. I don't date. I don't play little, what do you call them? Lovey-dovey games."

"I don't want to play games. I want you."

Jude pushed off from the door. Mary stared at her arms, wanting to trace the lines of her veins with her lips, wanting to feel the heavy weight of her breasts again, wanting to kiss away the strained look on her face.

"Go, Mary."

"But I—"

"Go."

"Can I see you again? If not here, then at the club?"

Jude looked incredulous. "Have you not heard me? There will be no seeing me."

"At Conquest. I will go there."

"No."

"Yes."

"No."

"Then you'll have to have them stop me." The words just jumped out and into a hurried sentence. Her heart was pounding as if her life depended upon seeing Jude. No meant certain death. And she'd fight like mad to make sure her heart kept beating.

"Why are you doing this?" Jude was watching her, eyes narrowed.

"Because I can't stop thinking about you and the way you made me feel." Her voice gave and she looked away. Emotion was welling in her chest, causing it to burn. When she looked back up at Jude, it was through tears. "I just can't stop."

A heavy silence fell over them. Mary had said her piece and yet the yearning and uncontrollable feelings were still churning inside. With Jude standing there in front of her, so close, she felt like she was going to combust if she didn't touch her.

Mary stared into her eyes, desperate to reach her. "Tell me you didn't feel the same. Tell me you haven't thought of me or that you truly don't ever want to see me again. Tell me that and I'll go." But just saying those words aloud threatened to shatter her. She'd fall to pieces right there in front of Jude with no way of putting herself back together again. The possibility terrified her, but she stood tall, willing to take the risk. If Jude didn't want to be with her again then she needed to know. But was there any way back from emotional death?

"Tell me."

Jude returned her stare, her face rock hard, showing no sign of what she was thinking or feeling. The pulse in her neck jumped, and Mary reached out to touch it. Jude caught her by the wrist and held her.

"Let me touch you," Mary said softly.

"I cannot." But Jude's voice, too, had changed, like a link in her strong chain of control had given.

Mary reached up with her other hand and brushed her hot cheek. Jude shuddered and caught her again by the wrist. Mary saw it then. The look she'd been dreaming about. It nearly melted her.

"Jude—"

But her words were muffled by a sudden move on Jude's part. Jude had turned and pressed her against the door, holding her hands captive over her head. After locking the door, she stared into Mary's eyes while struggling for breath.

"You want me," Jude said.

"Yes. More than anything. I—"

Jude smothered her mouth with her own, her lips so blissfully hot Mary nearly melted beneath her. She moaned at the contact, completely overwhelmed and surprised. This was what she'd dreamt of, longed for, and now that she had it she could hardly keep from fainting under Jude's kiss. "Jude," she said, sighing into her, wanting so much more.

Jude met her wish and granted it, pressing into her further and thrusting forward with her agile tongue. Mary returned the kiss and Jude took control again at once, capturing Mary's tongue and sucking on it, letting it slide in and out of her warm mouth. Then her own tongue came again, stronger than ever, exploring Mary with a vengeance, as if she and not Mary was the one clinging to life, completely dependent on their fiery physicality. Jude plunged back into her and released her wrist to shove her hand between her legs. Wearing a skirt, Mary opened her legs to allow her easier entry. Jude rubbed her fingers against Mary's aching flesh, touching her through her panties. Mary moaned into Jude's mouth, desperate for more. Jude answered by releasing her completely to hurriedly shove her skirt upward. Then, pulling away from the kiss, Jude eased her hand into Mary's panties.

"Wet," Jude said.

Mary cried out, loud and loaded with coiled erotic energy. Jude tensed and covered her mouth, then stuck her fingers over Mary's bottom teeth to rest on her tongue.

"Suck them," she whispered, staring into Mary's eyes. "Suck them while I touch you." And she rubbed her quicker, gliding her fingers along her clit, which was slick and coated with her wetness. Mary could feel it saturating, feel it pooling and touching her upper thighs. Each stroke seemed to milk more of it, and it was out of her control, coming forth in hot wave after wave. It was the same feeling she'd had at Conquest. Like her flesh needed Jude, wanted to consume her by wrapping itself around her. Mary's knees bent and her hips began to buck on their own accord. She groaned as she sucked on Jude's fingers.

"This is what you want?" Jude asked, her eyes fierce and beautiful.

Mary nodded.

Mary tried to groan and tried to speak, but Jude stopped her by pulling her fingers from her mouth. They were wet as they pressed against Mary's lips, silencing her.

"Shh. You must be quiet." She said this as her fingers slid inside Mary, hinging her. Mary shut her eyes while the fingers against her lips muffled her cry.

"Here," Jude said. "Like this." She lowered her hand from her mouth to grab Mary's. Then she pressed Mary's fingers to her lips where hers had just been. Mary opened her eyes and watched as Jude leaned in and licked her lips through her fingers, her other hand sliding up into her hole, again and again. Jude continued to kiss her, sucking her mouth in bits and pieces, lining Mary's fingers with her tongue. All the while the fucking continued, up and hard and slick until the small noises from Mary could no longer come, eaten up by the roughness of her pleasure-plowed throat.

"There it is," Jude said. "Take what you came for. Take it, Mary." She shoved upward with each word then engulfed Mary's mouth with her own. Harder and harder until Mary, losing all control of herself, grabbed Jude's head and held her to her as she came, coming in her mouth with a desperate, hungry tongue and struggling breaths.

She came, she came, she came, unable to get enough. As if Jude were an illusion and about to dissipate into the nothingness that was her life. She clung to her, with her hands and with her center, until Jude tore herself away, flushed and desperate for air. She stared at Mary for a few moments and then came at her again. The fierceness of her eyes had returned, wolf-like, locked in on her prey. She took Mary's hand and tugged her from the door. She spun her around and backed her to the desk where she cupped her hips and lifted her, bringing her to rest on piles of papers and files.

"Lie back," she said, pushing gently on her sternum. Mary eased back, her heart still hammering from the orgasm. Jude shoved upward on her skirt and wrapped her hands around her upper thighs to tug her forward. Then with one last hungry look, she pulled her panties aside and buried her face in her, heavily licking her soaked and overly sensitive flesh.

Panting, Mary held Jude's head and strained to watch as she was devoured first by Jude's tongue and then by her whole mouth. When she began to make noise, Jude reached up and plunged her fingers over Mary's bottom teeth again, easing them in and out as Mary sucked and Jude's mouth tugged. Files shifted beneath them; papers fell to the floor. Jude kept pushing, as if Mary were wriggling and hard to get hold of. Mary's legs trembled and her fingers tensed so hard they felt fused to Jude's head. Something else fell. It sounded like a keyboard. Jude started to hum and moved her head faster from side to side, pausing only for a millisecond to smack her lips away for a long breath. When she came back the last time, she once again shoved her fingers deep inside and pulsed five times hard and quick, sending Mary over instantly.

Mary lifted, her body stiff with pleasure, and she rocked like that, sucking on Jude's fingers as Jude fucked her and fed from her. Her insides tried to push out, her body tried to cave in around Jude. Her shoes fell from her feet. And still she rocked, suspended, floating through heaven. Longer and longer, so good, so good. And then it was gone, torn from her chest in a ragged, barely audible groan. She fell limp onto the desk and Jude eased up from between her legs. She could've lain there and enjoyed the post orgasmic bliss, but there was something else on her mind.

"Jude."

Mary sat up and watched as Jude began straightening her clothing. Mary stood and hurried to do the same. She adjusted her panties and fixed her blouse and skirt. She hurried to Jude and tried to kiss her. Jude did so only briefly, and Mary tried to touch her face, but Jude caught her wrist.

"What's wrong?" Mary asked. She searched Jude's blank but beautiful golden irises. Jude was gone. Already. That quickly. Mary panicked. "Jude?" She lowered her hand and pressed against Jude's covered flesh. Jude tensed, sucked in a rapid breath, and clenched her jaw. She tried to remove Mary's hand.

"Please let me touch you," Mary said. "Please. It's all I want."

"I thought you got what you wanted."

Mary shook her head. "Not all of it." She stroked Jude up and down, feeling the warmth of her flesh beneath her slacks. "Please."

Jude stopped her and her lashes fell closed over her eyes. Mary studied her and then removed her hand. When Jude looked up, Mary nearly gasped at the pain she saw swimming around her pupils.

"I cannot," Jude said sounding defeated and wounded. She backed away and unlocked the door. When she held it open, she looked back at Mary, the meaning clear.

"I don't want to go," Mary said, feeling her throat burn with tears. "I want you, Jude."

"Go, Mary," she whispered.

"Please."

Jude avoided her gaze and Mary felt the air take on a sudden chill, as if all their heated passion had simply breezed out the open door. Mary wanted to remain, to slam the door and hold Jude's face and tell her she would spend eternity getting to know her. That they had all the time in the world and that Mary wanted to please her, touch her, love her. That she would never stop. Never, ever stop.

"You must go," Jude said, forcing her back to reality.

Mary started to protest, but the phone on the desk rang. Jude released the door and stepped over to answer it. Her back was to Mary as she began speaking to someone in German. Mary stepped into her shoes, made her way to the door, waited, and when Jude didn't turn to see her off, she left and walked slowly into the fresh night.

CHAPTER SEVEN

Jude Jaeger wasn't the type to let her mind wander. But that was exactly what it was doing. Again and again it went to her past, replaying all the intense feelings she'd had during her previous relationship. Why now? But the answer was also the other subject taking up room in her mind. Mary. The woman was causing all sorts of turmoil in her normally guarded soul and she wasn't sure what it meant or what to do about it.

"Damn." She rose to face the window, folding her arms across her chest as she stared through the blinds into the sunny student parking lot. A few young men and women strolled toward their vehicles, heads down, heavy looking backpacks bowing their forms. It was a hot day and only the beginning of fall semester. She should have a million other things on her mind.

But there was only Mary.

"Hey, here's your green tea Frap."

Startled, Jude turned and studied her colleague with surprising poise considering she'd half expected it to be Mary, showing up like she had a couple days before, demanding to see her, to touch her, to reach in and stir her soul, while stirring her life into one huge mess. But it wasn't Mary and she had to get herself together. She offered a smile. "Thank you."

"No sweat." Her colleague Fran was a fellow teacher, tall and brunette with almond eyes. She taught French and Jude had known her for years. "You okay?"

Jude glanced down, noticed her own crossed arms, and lowered them. "I'm fine." She kept the smile and surprised herself and Fran both by inviting Fran to sit. "Please." She motioned toward one of the two chairs in front of her desk. Hopefully, some friendly conversation would keep her mind off Mary.

Fran settled in and sipped from her tall cup of coffee. She crossed her lean legs and Jude wondered, not for the first time, what she would be like to take in the heat of passion. She wondered the same about most attractive women and she felt safe in doing so. No one knew, and in the carnival of her mind, no one got involved or hurt or cheated on.

Which was how she liked things. Simple, uninvolved, efficient. But her mind wasn't functioning so simply anymore. Images of Fran quickly bled into images of Mary coming all over her fingers as she fucked her up against the door.

"Jude?" Fran was looking at her, having obviously said something.

"Hmm?"

"Are you sure you're okay?"

Jude forced herself to sit. She sipped her Frappuccino but suddenly didn't want it. Her stomach felt like it was churning battery acid. "I'm fine," she said again. But the clock on her wall told her it was ten minutes until the start of Mary's class. She would be on campus now, possibly lingering. Her gaze drifted to the open door for the umpteenth time that afternoon. But there was no one there, just the quiet hallway.

"I'm used to you being a little reserved, but flat-out ignoring me is something I have to take offense to." Fran was smiling, teasing. "But seriously, Jude, what's going on? You look like someone just punched you in the gut."

Funnily enough, that's exactly how she felt. Mary had been a sucker punch to her abdomen. The kind Harry Houdini died from. She swallowed hard as she thought about it. Houdini was the master of escape. But even he succumbed to the sucker punch, unable to escape his own cruel destiny. What made her so sure she could escape hers, whatever it may be?

"Jude?"

Because I make my own destiny.

Which was why she had rules. Why she never told anyone at Conquest her name, why she usually never let anyone touch her—

Fran was eyeing her, one brow arched, and Jude had to interrupt her own self-berating.

"I feel a little…" But there were no words, just more images. Mary.

Up against the door, on the desk, sucking on her fingers, moaning, standing there with that sweet, sweet desperately hungry look.

"Ill?"

"Yes." Why had she fucked her in her office? She'd broken a cardinal rule. Never outside the club and never again if they were too clingy.

"Maybe you should go home. Call it a day?"

She refocused on Fran instead of staring at the short stack of files she and Mary had slid to the floor just days before. "I cannot." Her eyes nearly fluttered closed. She'd said the same to Mary. Just like that. All soft and sad, like she could barely get the words out.

"Well, you need to do something. You look like you're going to pass out. How many classes do you have left? I could cover for you."

"I need to check in on Guadalupe's Spanish class and then I plan on going home." She didn't want to check on that particular class, knowing Mary would be there, but she had to do her job. Besides, Mary hadn't come to find her again so maybe she'd finally taken the hint. But would seeing her bring her running back?

If I'm this bad with thinking about Mary, just how much is Mary thinking of me?

"You sure?"

"Yes."

Fran set down her cup of coffee and folded her hands in her lap. She sat and stared at Jude.

This was why Jude tried not to spend an extended amount of time with her. Fran was a silent sleuth. Long, drawn out moments of silence didn't bother her, and she'd hold Jude's stare for several minutes at a time, waiting, searching, analyzing.

It was like being under a fucking microscope. One that could see into her emotions as well as her cells.

Jude had to claw out of it before the heavy beam of Fran's eyes weighed her down.

Shouldering out of her cream blazer, she tried to change her tone and sound upbeat. "The first week of classes is always difficult."

Fran replied quickly but didn't move, her eyes still waiting. "I know. I can't believe August is here already. I swear it's the devil's month. At least it is in Phoenix."

"Yes." Jude grabbed a file and pretended to organize her desk. The silence was maddening.

One minute.

Two minutes.

Fran was unwavering.

Jude continued to push around files and class workbooks, her insides burning, reliving what she'd done to Mary on the desk. The images just kept coming, and she was sure Fran could see them, like a short movie on old film, clipped and stuttering, one-second shots of her and Mary in different embraces.

Jude cleared her throat, thanked whatever gods there were in the heavens she wasn't the type to blush, and then checked the doorway. This time Fran followed her line of sight and looked over her shoulder. The hallway was still empty with only the muffled sound of two others talking a few doors down. When Fran returned to her original position, one in which she was looking dead at Jude, she was slow to do so.

"Expecting someone?"

Jude reached for the Frap with the urge to occupy her mouth. "Hmm? No."

"Are you sure? Because I can come back later."

Jude sipped heartily and shook her head. She needed Fran to stop asking questions. The cup tipped as she returned it to her blotter. Standing, she righted the cup and Fran tried to help clean, but Jude shooed her hands away, wiping up the bit of whipped cream and frozen green tea quickly with a napkin she had in her desk.

I should keep the door closed. Closed and locked. Like I did after she left.

"Jude."

She stilled. Fran had gently clasped her wrist. She appeared concerned, her classically beautiful face washed out with worry, her eyes larger than usual.

"I'm fine," Jude said automatically. But this time she felt her cheeks heat and her pulse race. Being under the microscope was getting to her regardless of her proud resolve.

"Yeah, I know. You're fine," she said carefully, as if she understood and knew it had to be something they couldn't speak loudly about. "Please get some rest." She gave Jude's wrist one last squeeze and turned and left, leaving Jude standing alone behind her desk, cold, soaked napkin in hand. She threw it away and sank into her chair. This wasn't like her. Wasn't like her at all. She was always the picture of poise no matter what the situation.

She'd have to apologize to Fran even though she knew she wouldn't be able to come up with a reasonable excuse. Her own behavior had never upset her before or caused her to worry about explaining herself to others. It was no wonder Fran was concerned. She was behaving like a paranoid imbecile.

With her head in her hands, she forced herself to take several deep breaths. The air straightened her back and helped to clear her mind. Everything was fine and was going to remain fine. She'd just made one mistake, that was all. She grabbed her blazer and shoulder bag. The Spanish class had already started, and she hoped she could just slip in and sit for a while. As she strode toward the class, she kept her eyes focused on her path. She didn't look for Mary, nor did she anticipate her stepping into view. She just kept everything calm and smooth with her head held high just as she always did. Today was just like any other day and she had to check on this new Spanish teacher.

The back door to the classroom eased open quite noiselessly when she entered, allowing her a stealthy entry. A few students turned and eyed her as she slid into a desk in the last row. The class was going over an assignment, and the instructor was calling on a different student for each answer. Jude plucked out her pen and notebook and began making notes. The instructor had the class under control and he was doing well with explaining each answer. Jude crossed her legs, settling in.

She didn't see Mary right away and she didn't allow herself to look for her either. She told herself it didn't matter and that Mary was just another student. But despite her calm manner, which lasted all of ten minutes, her spine tingled when she heard him call for Mary. And it felt like every hair on her body rose when she heard Mary answer.

Jude scanned the classroom and found her several rows in front of her and toward the right. If Mary looked over her left shoulder, she'd have a clear line of sight to Jude. Thankfully, she didn't. The instructor praised her for the correct answer and moved on. Jude's eyes, however, remained fixed on her.

Mary was busy writing something in a notebook. Her hair was down and it seemed to shimmer under the fluorescent lights. It was the color of a desert brook with different shades of brown sparkling under the sun as it flowed. Jude recalled the way it smelled like jasmine and how it mixed with an earthy sweat when she was hot with passion.

Mary scratched her cheek and Jude eyed her fingers and traced down her arm with her gaze. She studied her blouse, which was red and lead down to dark slacks. How many buttons did the blouse have? Could she rip them all open with one lustful tear like she had at Conquest? She'd had to give Mary a T-shirt to wear home that night. She wondered if she still had it, wondered if she slept in it.

Mary tucked a strand of hair behind her ear and Jude saw the side of her face and a delicate slice of neck. She knew how it tasted, how it quivered and gave slightly beneath her teeth while Mary cried out in her ear.

Those cries, so fervent and virginal. Like no one on earth had ever touched her or tasted her before. Like Jude was some celestial body coming down from the heavens to ravish her. Mary, open and dripping with hot arousal before Jude even laid a finger on her.

Jude couldn't make herself look away. Mary was completely captivating. Jude's body was reacting and she forced her mind from the desire she felt for her to the reasons why. Why did Mary like her so much? Was it because she really was virginal and Jude just happened to be the one to touch her? If so, then Mary was simply confused, caught up in her first experience with a woman. It happened all the time.

Women had liked her before, but usually it had to do with those first time feelings and she'd been able to ward them off quickly. Most had understood it was just for fun and only at the club. But none of them had been as persistent and as persuasive as Mary. And none of them had brought up feelings of the past, forcing her to recall every single spark of lust and every single stab of rejection. But Mary did and Jude shoved away the painful recollection of being used and cast aside by her ex to concentrate on the more beautiful sight before her, deciding to focus on the lust rather than the pain.

Jude watched Mary closely, knowing she was more beautiful than any woman she'd ever been with. She wanted to talk to her, nuzzle her hair and neck. Lick the soft hairs near her ear to make her shudder.

Mary turned a little then as if she weren't quite sure if someone had whispered her name. Jude held her breath and studied the side of her face. Her cheeks colored as she seemed to wait for the whisper to come again, staring at the side wall. Jude knew then that Mary could feel her stare, feel it like her fingers had just brushed along her jaw.

And then her eyes shifted and she turned some more, melting a gaze right into Jude. Like a shot of strong whiskey, Mary's eyes burned her insides and Jude wanted to run right for her and slam her with a powerful, all-consuming kiss. Mary seemed to see that in her gaze because her mouth fell open at first with surprise and then it set with that desperate, hungry look, telling Jude, "Yes, come on. I want it."

Jude stiffened, trying to get control of herself. It was impossible, the whole thing maddening, and Jude knew it. She was only torturing them both. Hurriedly, she rose and left the room, shoving her notes and pen in her shoulder bag as she went. She crossed the lawn and headed toward the parking lot.

She couldn't do this with Mary, or anyone. It only led to hurt and betrayal, one always wanting more than the other. And she wasn't about to go through that again.

When she heard Mary calling after her, she quickened her pace and didn't dare look back.

But her mind kept repeating over and over again as she drove, "Mary."

CHAPTER EIGHT

Mary sat staring at the phone while gnawing on the cuticle of her middle finger.

Call her.

It was a never ending mantra in her mind. Call her call her call her.

"Agh!" She picked up the receiver and pressed the speed dial. The line to Conquest rang and rang. It was ten p.m. and she'd already called three times and hung up before anyone could answer. This time, though, the gruff man from before answered and she had to cover the phone for a moment before she could speak.

"Yeah?" he said. "Hello?"

"Right, hello," she said, her voice sounding annoying even to her.

"Can I speak with Jude please?"

There was a crunching noise, like maybe he was eating ice. "Jude?"

"Yes, Jude Jaeger."

"There ain't no one here by that name."

Mary was baffled for a second. It had never occurred to her that those that frequented Conquest like Jude might not know her name.

"Uh, she's the tall blonde—"

"She's busy."

"Sorry?"

"She's busy."

"Well, can you give her a message?"

"Look, lady. You called here before, huh?"

He didn't give her time to answer.

"We ain't a doctor's office and we ain't an answering service."

"Well, how…how does one see her…if they should want to."

"You come in. If she wants you, you'll know."

"And if she doesn't?"

"You'll know that too. Have a nice night."

The click turned into an angry dial tone and she pulled the phone away to grimace at it before turning it off. It was as she'd suspected. She would have to go to Conquest herself if she wanted to see Jude.

It didn't help her nerves any, and she still wasn't quite sure what she was going to do. She'd been all ready to go to Conquest the other evening, ready and determined to confront Jude and declare her feelings. But after their tryst in Jude's office, things weren't so clear anymore. Jude had taken her and it had been beyond her fantasies, but she'd also closed off from her, telling her she couldn't see her.

She attacked the same poor cuticle again as she stood and paced. Her head kept telling her to call and her heart kept telling her to see her. But the part of her that worried, the part she couldn't ever seem to pin down to a specific area, that part was cautioning her, telling her not to be the fool.

But a fool was what she already felt like. A stalker was the label she was headed for. How would she feel if some creep kept coming on to her, calling and showing up demanding to be seen? She'd call the cops, no questions asked.

So why was she doing this?

Because I can't stop.

Great. Maybe she was a stalker. Someone unable to stop her insane behavior.

She stopped and massaged her temples. The confusion lay with Jude. Why did she take her in her office if she didn't want her? To get rid of her? That wasn't likely, was it? Did Jude fuck those she wanted to get rid of? The way she fucked, it didn't seem likely. It would only make people want to stay.

Jude had wanted to take her. She felt it in her touch, saw it in her eyes, heard it in her voice.

She'd seen it and felt it earlier today in the classroom too. The way Jude was looking at her, like she wanted to take her right then and there. There was definitely an attraction.

They had fused. But Jude was fighting it.

She groaned and crossed the hall to her bedroom. If only she could stop thinking about her. If only…

She stripped and crawled into bed. After extinguishing the light she moved her hand down to between her legs. That pressure was there, constant and pulsing, forcing her body to pay attention. She could remember feeling something similar in her teens, but she'd never done much about it. She'd been raised to think that touching oneself in an erotic way was bad and even disturbing. Only those with serious issues did such things, and bad things would happen to them because of it. The gist of it had been aimed at boys, but girls took it to heart too. The vagina was no man's land, and no one had better be touching it, boy or girl.

So she'd left herself virtually unexplored. She'd been with a couple of men and they'd tried to do things to her, but she'd been so turned off by their bodies and actions she'd hardly thought of her own needs. She'd just wanted the situation over with so they'd leave. If having to go through the relentless pawing and throat-clogging tongue kissing was what it meant to make love and have an orgasm, she'd just as soon skip it. And she had.

Until Jude.

She closed her eyes and began to touch herself. Her body relaxed and a deep sigh fell over her as her fingers traced through her light hairs to her calling flesh. She sighed again as she found her cleft and surrounded it with pressing fingertips. Jude's face came to mind and she gyrated her hand, slowly at first and then with greater pressure and speed. She moaned as she remembered the way Jude had kissed her up against the door, rimming her fingers with her tongue and hungry lips. She remembered the way she'd plunged fingers deep inside, making her come all over her hand. And then finally, she remembered Jude's hot mouth fastened to her flesh, licking and taking, licking and taking.

Oh, sweet fuck, yes.

She'd never felt so alive, like she was electricity humming through a wire. Never to stop flowing.

Never. Never.

She panted and began to call Jude's name. Yes. Yes.

She had her now and had her power. It was in her hand and in her mind.

And it was really fucking good.

She cried out and sat halfway up as the orgasm took hold of her. The ceiling ebbed and flowed for a long while as she rocked there in that state. When she finally fell back on the bed, her breathing felt clear and raw like it did after a good run, and she realized she'd just given herself a gift she'd been denying for far too long.

Jude. Where have you been all my life?

CHAPTER NINE

The woman was writhing beneath her, begging for it, digging her nails into Jude's back. Jude closed her eyes and tried to concentrate on the moment and the woman, but her head wasn't in it. When she did manage to focus on her, all she did was notice the unpleasant things about her.

Her skin smelled sickly sweet, like she'd put on way too much scented lotion. It reminded Jude of her great-aunt and the way she'd worn way too much lotion the last few years of her life. Jude shook her head to try to get the thought from her mind. She flexed her hips harder and quicker, pumping the woman insanely. She would make her come and be done with her. There was no way she was doing anything else with her. Not this one. Not tonight.

The woman screamed loudly as she came, and the harsh noise from it made Jude's ear ring.

Crawling from her, Jude looked down at her and tried hard to find the sight hot and satisfying. The woman was on her back, legs splayed, round tits buoying on her chest as she giggled. Her heavy makeup was melting off her face with her sweat. She looked like a macabre Barbie doll and Jude had to look away.

She busied herself removing the condom and the dildo as the woman rose and dressed.

"That was some fuck, baby," the woman said, sounding like a keyed up schoolgirl, one way too young for her realistic age of forty-five-ish. "You do that kind of thing all the time, or am I just special?"

Jude sat and wiped the dildo with antiseptic wipes. Christ, now the insecurity questions as well? Was I good? Your best? Have you had better? "You are special," she said with no inflection to her voice. The woman ate it up and even squeaked a little.

"I wish my husband could fuck like that. But he always shoots way too early."

Jude stopped her. "Nein. No more."

The woman closed her mouth and then smiled. "Okay. I don't blame you, really. I wouldn't want to hear all—"

Jude rose and slipped the straps off her hips. She'd remained fully clothed, and she was especially glad she had. It took less time to get rid of the woman and assured her cardinal rule of no touching would be followed.

"You can go," she said, holding the door for her. She was usually a little friendlier, wanting the women to leave on pleasant terms. Pleasure was, after all, what the whole thing was about. But she found that she didn't care with this woman and she wondered why she'd fucked her at all.

To rid my mind of—

The woman was attractive enough, on a popular society scale, and she'd been more than eager and willing. But Jude had found the whole encounter boring and predictable.

Blonde woman with boobs is flirtatious. Blonde woman with boobs gives herself over easily. Blonde woman with boobs makes high-pitched squeaky noises of pleasure. Blonde woman with boobs says things like, "Yes! Oh, give it to me good, baby doll!" Blonde woman with boobs comes, breaks at least two fake nails on Jude's back, and then lays there humming.

Now the blonde woman with boobs was giving her a knowing and secretive smile. Her hand skimmed Jude's cheek and she stood on her toes to kiss her softly on the mouth. When Jude didn't respond with movement of her own lips, the woman simply backed away and gave her a wink. She walked away without any further comment, slinging a massive purse over her shoulder, their brief encounter obviously not very meaningful for her either. It was what it was. Short. Right to the point. No strings.

Jude closed the door and continued to clean herself up. Perhaps she was being too cynical. She'd never really thought this much about her encounters before. As she wiped her face and neck with a cleansing wipe, she knew the reason for the sudden change. But she wasn't allowing herself to go there. She would just keep doing what she was doing. Someone was bound to come along and shake up her world a little. Get things back on track.

After adjusting her hair and rinsing her mouth with a bit of vodka, she sprayed on some cologne and remade her bed, replacing the soft blanket the blonde woman with boobs had lain on. And as she thought about it, she knew that two weeks ago she'd have found at least some pleasure in making the woman call her a baby doll. In fact, she probably would've loved it, fucking her at least three times just to hear it.

She straightened her back and eyed her reflection. She looked the same. Stoic, almost rigid, with a god-like bone structure and spiked blond hair. But she was paler than usual with dark brushstrokes under her eyes. They were perfectly shaped, like someone had held her head and swept a delicate paintbrush beneath them, leaving a perfectly shaped mark.

Lack of sunlight was probably the cause. She hadn't been getting out much. Hadn't felt like taking her evening hikes after work. All she'd been concerned about was work and coming to

Conquest. The rest would have to wait until she felt more like herself again. She could only hope it would be soon.

She opened the door and waited, cocking her head to listen to the muted voices. There were groans, moans, laughter, and the snapping of whips or crops or something leather. The hallway was nearly empty, though, with only two bodies tangled into each other toward the end.

Jude braved a step and then walked faster, pissed at herself for being so damn paranoid. She strode to the end of the hall and turned to face the main room. Her heart leapt and fell in a split second. A woman was standing near the door. She was short with brown hair. For a moment, Jude thought it was Mary. And for a moment, she nearly died with fear and excitement.

She was breathing freely with relief when she felt a cold, rough hand on her shoulder. She jerked a little and Cord removed his hand, obviously worried about startling her.

He was quick to report, probably seeing the angry look on her face.

"Yeah, sorry, didn't mean to scare ya." He was sweaty like always, as if his job consisted of standing over a grill for hours at a time. She waited for his point.

"Thought you'd want to know that lady called again."

She refused to blink or to show any sign of recognition.

"She asked to talk to you and said something about coming here to see you."

When she still didn't respond, he hurriedly finished.

"I told her, I says look, this ain't a doctor's office and I ain't no answering service." He laughed a little, amused at himself. His smile fell when he once again met her gaze.

"Well, okay then."

He left her then and headed back behind the bar. She stood a moment longer, her insides rushing with adrenaline. Mary might come. She had called again.

Fuck.

She clenched her jaw and walked up to the woman by the door.

"Hello," she said, smelling the virgin on her at once.

"Hi."

"Would you like to come back with me and get more… comfortable? I promise I won't bite."

The woman laughed, full of nerves.

"I'm here to see—" She held up the card.

Jude moved away. The woman was taken and off-limits. Fuming, Jude stalked to the bar and ordered a shot of vodka.

What the hell was she going to do? Sit and twiddle her thumbs all night while she worried and waited for a previous fuck to show? That wasn't like her and the whole point of tonight and the few nights previous were to keep her mind off—

She refused to think of her name.

Why couldn't she just move the fuck on and not worry about it? So what if she showed up? She'd tell her to fuck off and continue to move on.

The shot glass felt cool in her hand and she downed the liquid quickly with a snap of her head. It burned so lovely she considered another.

Behind her, the main door opened and the men on the barstools next to her did their general turn and stare. She didn't bother.

Cord took her glass and stared at her. She played it off at first, but when his eyes kept shifting to the door, she forced down the sudden lump in her throat and turned.

Another brunette, the same height as the other had entered. She was standing right next to her, face hidden in the shadows. Jude's heart leapt again and beat insanely within her chest.

It was just a trick. It wasn't her. Just another woman who resembled her. Calm down.

But the woman stepped forward and spoke, sending Jude's heart and stomach into a spinning deadfall.

"Hello, Jude."

It took a moment for Jude to react. When she did it was quick and sharp and she grabbed Mary by the hand to lead her away from the others. Mary stumbled along willingly, talking the entire time.

"I'm glad you're here. I didn't think you would see me. Thank—"

Jude reached her door and turned, covering her mouth quite forcefully.

"Do not say my name!" She lowered her hand as it started to tremble with her anger. She jerked Mary into the room and slammed the door. Mary stood looking shocked, and she shook her head and tried to explain.

"I'm sorry. I—"

"Enough!" Jude ran her hands through her hair and slapped them on her thighs in frustration. She wanted to scream at her. How dare she come here when she'd been told not to. How dare she insist on seeing her, acting like a harmless little schoolgirl who doesn't know any better. How dare she use her name in front of the others!

"I am so angry," Jude said. "So, so angry. You have no idea, do you?"

"I—"

"I've heard enough from you, Mary. Mary with your pretend innocence and insistent little attitude."

Mary stared at her for a long moment. "Why are you so angry?"

Jude wanted to laugh but she was too shocked to do so. "Why? Why do you think? Because you keep showing up." Jude groaned in frustration as her plan to tell Mary to fuck off floated away. Nothing, it seemed, was simple when it came to Mary.

Mary's face reddened, and for a second Jude thought it would crack and she would cry. But instead it contorted into obvious anger.

"You think I want to bother you? Like this is some game and I'm—I'm getting off on it?"

"Are you not?"

"No!"

"Then why?"

Mary grew still and stared at her again. The anger slowly fell from her face and her body went slack. She seemed to have trouble breathing and Jude again feared she would cry. A twinge of guilt tried to make itself known, but she wouldn't have it. A twinge of surprise and panic came as Mary moved toward the door.

"What are you doing?" Jude asked, more confused than ever.

Mary didn't answer, just reached for the doorknob.

Jude pressed her own hand to the door, holding it closed.

"I'm trying to leave," Mary said, avoiding her gaze. Her voice was a whisper of defeat.

Jude inhaled deeply, the statement causing her body to continue to react. Her heart raced and she felt what she could only guess was disappointment and the fear of loss rushing through her. She pressed harder on the door.

"No."

Mary finally looked at her. Her eyes were liquid with tears.

"Don't do this," she said, her voice barely audible. "Just let me go."

"I cannot," Jude said, her own throat tightening. She cringed at her own words.

"You told me you don't want me to come to you. I get it now."

Jude struggled for words. "Why did you not get it before?"

"Because a part of me wanted to believe you wanted me. Despite what you said."

Jude fought for control within herself. Mary knew. She had felt it. She knew Jude wanted her.

Let her go. Let her go and this can all be over.

But her hand remained pressed against the door and her heart continued to thud madly and hotly within her chest. She inhaled again, struggling for the strength to ease away from the door.

"Jude," Mary said. "Let me go. Please, before I break down." Her breath shook with tears. She held out Jude's T-shirt, having had it tucked under her arm.

Jude inched closer, bleeding inside for causing her pain. She felt her nostrils flare as she imagined Mary's scent marking her shirt after having slept in it all curled and warm in her bed.

"Mary." She cupped her jaw and smoothed her thumb under her eye. Mary trembled and blinked away the hurt. Her skin grew hot and her eyes were serious with want.

Jude was lost now. Captivated. She wanted to kiss her. To hold her warm lips with her own, tasting again and again. She pulled her closer and lowered her hand to embrace her. She was a blissful inch from her mouth when a banging came from the door.

Mary jerked and backed away and Jude angrily opened it, expecting to find Cord relaying Mary's presence to her even though she was obviously already well aware.

"Hi." It was one of her regulars, dressed in a leather vest and faded jeans. Her crooked smile and heavy lidded eyes said she was ready and willing to go, but Jude wanted nothing to do with the ride.

"I am busy."

The woman showed surprise and then caught sight of Mary. "Oh." Her eyes drifted back to Jude. "The sign says go, so I thought—"

"The sign is wrong."

"Okay. I can wait."

She leaned in a little as if trying to lure Jude further. Jude tried to close the door, but Mary squeezed through.

"Excuse me," she said, breezing past the woman. Jude shouldered past her as well and hurried after Mary.

"Wait. Mary, wait."

She was able to catch her gently by the arm as they stopped in a dark corner. Around them the thump of the music did its best to muffle out the laughter and moans coming from the walls. A threesome was getting it on near the bar, and Jude watched as Mary stared at them, arms crossed over her chest.

"You're free," she said, obviously detached from Jude and the moment they had shared just moments before. "She's waiting for you."

"Come back with me." Jude tried to tilt her face toward her, but Mary refused.

"She's what you want isn't she? Just a hot fuck."

Jude felt stricken but she wasn't sure why. The truth was the truth.

Mary took her silence as an answer. "I thought so." She crossed to the door and Jude called for her one last time. As she turned, Jude felt the other woman tug on her arm. Mary saw it too, and when Jude made no move to get away from her, Mary walked through the door leaving only the warm evening breeze behind her.

CHAPTER TEN

Mary answered the ringing phone lines one after the other. She thanked each person for calling and then placed them on hold. It was Monday, and Monday, as they say, was a bitch.

"Thank you for holding, how can I help you?" She began typing in the client's account information as he relayed his problem. It was typical Monday morning mumbo jumbo, and she was able to work through the calls quickly.

The calls, though, were the least of her problems, and she wished more would come in so she couldn't think about anything else. But co-worker asshole number two was back again and leaning over her cubicle.

"Hey, Mary. Remember eight is late."

She'd shown up at eight fifteen and it seemed everyone and their mother had noticed. She wanted to groan. She was always on time. Always.

She covered her mouthpiece and leaned toward him. "I clock in at seven fifty-eight every morning. Do you?"

He didn't. He was notoriously late, which, she figured, was why he was picking on her.

His cheesy smile vanished, but he didn't leave. "Don't get your panties in a wad just because you're late today, Mary."

She glared at him. What an ass. His thick arms dangled over her wall and she thought about grabbing them and pulling down hard. Would he shriek? Yell? Curse? Cry?

"I'm just trying to help you out." He smacked his gum, or whatever it was he was chewing, loudly. He had a tiny drink straw tucked behind his ear and he smelled like too much cologne mixed with coffee.

To her dismay, he continued to hang there while she finished her call.

"Hey," he said softer, like he was telling her a secret. "We're gonna get together later in the week. Go back to that club we were telling you about."

She couldn't help but laugh aloud and he looked a little nervous for a second.

"Yeah," he said. "What's so funny?"

"Nothing." She swallowed her laughter with a bit of coffee. "Let me know the details." She rose and rounded her cubicle area so that she was standing directly next to him. He turned from the wall and stared at her. She knew he and the others were still somewhat surprised by her emerging new I-don't-give-a-fuck attitude, and she couldn't help but gloat about it. The last time they'd spoken he'd insulted her while she did nothing.

Well, not today.

Inching closer to him she said, "You name the time, big boy. I know some guys there who will really rock your world."

He drew back and blinked. She pursed her lips at him as if in a silent kiss, and then she left him to stride into the restroom. The room was quiet as she entered, like a great cathedral to all things pure and pristine. She barely made it to the far stall before she burst into tears. Huddled there on the toilet, she cried into her hands, trying to stifle her sobs.

Her life was over. Just as it had finally begun. She'd met Jude and her soul had awakened. Life had a sun and a blue sky and beautiful and erotic thoughts and feelings. It felt glorious and exciting, as if she'd been saturated in ecstasy and awe. She'd imagined herself dipped in it, like an apple dipped and dripping with caramel. The apple becoming sweeter, delicious and more tempting.

She tore off a few stubborn pieces of toilet paper and dabbed at her eyes. She'd thought *she'd* been sweeter and delicious and more tempting. She'd felt that way. And she'd thought Jude had too.

But it had all been a game. Conquest itself was a game. No one went there for passionate lovemaking and soul-awakening connections. They went there for sex and pleasure and kinky S and M things she knew nothing about. Jude was a part of it all. She was there specifically for those reasons. Nothing else.

Mary had been ridiculous, trying as many times as she had. God, what a fool. She was lucky Jude had been as patient as she had.

And yet...

She couldn't get past that look in Jude's eyes. It was attraction, yes. Lust. She'd felt it for Jude; Jude had felt it in return. But that's all it was, nothing more. And she had to let it go.

So why couldn't she?

She mulled it over just as she had every night after that first encounter. The answer was there, right in front of her, but it was difficult to accept. Really difficult considering the way Jude had behaved.

But it was there and she couldn't deny it.

She felt more than just lust for Jude. She felt so many powerful things.

The main door to the restroom opened and she stood as two women entered. She knew who they were but hadn't cared enough to learn their names. One of them, she'd actually considered befriending.

"Did you hear what Carla said?"

"About Mary?"

"Yes, can you believe it? She's actually being a bitch."

"I didn't think she had it in her."

Water ran from the row of sinks as Mary rested her head against the stall door to listen.

"Oh, I did. I always knew she was a bitch. She just never spoke."

"I don't know. I thought she was kind of…sad."

"Please."

"No really. She seemed really sad and sort of lonely. Like she lived alone with twenty-five cats or something."

"I'll tell you what's sad. Her wardrobe. She dresses like a Bible salesman."

They laughed.

"Her cardigans are cute."

"No way. The cardigans are so Mr. Rogers."

More laughter.

"You're the one being a bitch now."

"So? At least I can. When you have a body like this you're allowed to be a bitch. I own it. Have you ever seen a tighter ass?" She clawed at the mirror like a cat. "That's right. Look but don't touch. Eat your heart out, boys."

"You're disgusting." They both leaned toward the mirror to touch up their mascara. "I think Mary's just misunderstood."

"You're a dyke."

"Shut up!"

"You are. Just like she is."

"She is not. Is she?"

The woman shrugged and retrieved her lipstick. "Probably. She told Bobby today that she knew some guys at that club who would really rock his world."

"What?"

"As in gay sex. Yeah. She totally did. She's probably into all kinds of kinky shit. The quiet ones always are."

"Wow." The other woman grew quiet. "I thought that whole thing was a joke. I didn't think she even showed."

"Well, apparently she did. She'd probably been going all along."

Mary closed her eyes and wiped the stray tears from her cheeks. The women left and she heard the door bang behind them. She studied her reflection as she walked to the sink. They were right. She looked plain, unremarkable. Like she had twenty-five cats at home and no one else in her life to talk to. Her dark blue Oxford was neatly pressed and dreary, leading into black slacks. The cardigan hugging her desk chair was tan and nearly worn through. She rarely did speak while at work, and honestly, it wasn't because everyone was an ass or a stuck up bitch.

It was her. Mary.

Mary, Mary quite contrary.

How does your garden grow?

She winced, having heard the rhyme mimicked to her her entire life. Every time someone sang it to her, she'd retreated further and further into her shell.

People were mean.

Uncaring.

Harsh.

Cruel.

Not just to her, but to everyone. Those that prevailed either didn't care, had no heart, or were really good looking. Everyone else was shark chum. She'd learned that lesson early on in life, and she'd done her best to steer clear of the bloody waters.

But here she was again, doing all she could to avoid the hungry predators. Yet somehow, they were circling, having caught her scent.

Avoidance wasn't working. Living a lonely, sexually and emotionally unfulfilling life wasn't working.

Something had to be done.

People be damned.

Chapter Eleven

Jude was late and it was really bothering her. She was always prompt, even when arriving to Conquest. Her life was like her ledger—precise, perfect, and no room for error. She cursed as she tried to unlock the private entrance to the club. Night was falling faster now and they desperately needed a light by the door, but no one was opting for it but her. Cord, she guessed, probably lived in an alley somewhere, so lights wouldn't be his thing.

He gave her a curious eye as she entered. "Thought for a second you weren't coming."

"Maybe thinking isn't your thing."

He set down the shot glass he was polishing and instead rubbed his hands with the towel. He had a bin full of glasses, readying them for the bar. The back room was stifling, small, and dim, the pounding of the club sounding like a cacophony around them.

"You got something you wanna say?"

It was funny how some people confronted her. Some got right in her face. Some did it passively. Some shook in their boots and looked her dead in the eyes. She'd never expected to have this sort of conversation with Cord, but here he was, doing his best to square off with her.

"No."

He pushed his shoulders back a little. "Okay, then."

"Yeah."

"Hey." He pointed a finger at her. "If you don't wanna come anymore, you don't have to."

She dropped her duffel bag. "What?"

"I won't ask any questions."

"What?"

He sighed. "Sometimes people need a break."

She felt her stomach twist painfully inside. What the fuck was he saying? "I don't."

"Sometimes people just have enough. Ya know?"

"No."

"I'm just sayin' if you—"

"Jesus Christ." She grabbed her bag.

"You don't seem like you wanna be here is all."

She hurried past him and heard him call out, "I ain't the only one that's noticed."

There were people in the main room and a few standing at the bar, but she didn't bother to check them out. Cord called out something else, and she knew he'd followed her out to the bar. She waved him off, her ears already on fire with his words.

Didn't want to be there? Where did he come up with that? She'd just had two women together night before last. And her regulars were pouring in just as they always had.

He was crazy.

Fucking Cord.

But as she set her bag down to unlock her door, tiny pins pricked the back of her mind. She hadn't been enjoying the conquering like she usually did.

No.

Just stop.

She did enjoy it. She just didn't enjoy it with every woman.

"Fuck me!" Her key didn't seem to be turning right. She turned the knob and the door eased open.

The lamps were on and someone was on her bed.

Mary.

Jude blinked, unsure if what she was seeing were real. She tried to react in anger, but her throat tightened as Mary moved and stood at the end of the bed. Her brown hair hung down past her shoulders where it rested on a white Oxford shirt. The shirt was unbuttoned a good ways and tied in a knot at her sternum, showing off her abdomen and a black lacy bra. The trail of her smooth, pale torso led to a black mini skirt and black thigh-high stockings. Black stiletto heels glimmered in the light as she walked very slowly up to Jude.

"Aren't you going to close the door?"

"What are you doing?" Jude finally managed to ask.

"Close the door and you'll see." Instead of waiting for Jude to do it, Mary brushed by her, slid the sign to red, and closed the door. She tugged on Jude's shirt as she headed back to the bed, giving her a dangerously sexy look over her shoulder as she did so.

Jude started to speak, but Mary stopped her. "I know you're wondering why I'm here since you made it clear I shouldn't come around anymore." She drug over a chair Jude kept in the corner and encouraged Jude to sit. Jude chose to stand.

"I've been doing some thinking, and I realized, hey, this Jude person, she's just into fucking. That's all. I shouldn't take offense at that or get all hurt over it. Right?"

She returned to the bed and pulled back the covers. Two different sized dildos and an electric massager were on the sheets along with a small bottle of lube.

Mary kicked off her stilettos and crawled onto the bed. She sat on her knees and looked at Jude.

"So I decided to come here tonight and thank you."

Jude was at a complete loss. Mary, there and waiting, wearing an outfit that would make any woman drop down to her knees in worship.

"For what?" she almost whispered.

"For awakening me."

Slowly, she began inching up her skirt to reveal more pale flesh leading to pink, none of it covered by panties. "Please sit, Jude. I don't want you to touch me. I just want you to watch. I want to show you what you've done for me."

Jude hesitated. She wasn't in control and it made her uncomfortable. But Mary was unlike anything she'd ever seen, and she was on her bed, slipping her fingers into her already glistening folds.

"This isn't a trick, Jude. It's just me, touching myself in front of you. Nothing more. I don't expect anything more, and I won't. I just want to fuck." She sighed as her fingers found her clit and Jude heated and slid down into the chair.

Jude could smell the jasmine of her moist skin and as she watched, she swore she could feel her hot, slippery flesh.

"Something's happened to me, Jude. Since that first night we met. My clit, it throbs now. Aches. It wants to be touched, licked, sucked. All the time. And my skin..." She rubbed her hand over her breast and up along her neck. "It's the same. It burns for touch."

Jude swallowed and tried to steady her breathing. A cool sweat had broken along her brow and her flesh was beginning to throb. She wasn't sure if she could take this. Mary was luring her in, more so than ever, leaving her helpless to fight it.

She should ask her to leave.

Before it went any further.

But Mary was playing by Jude's rules now, and an excuse wouldn't be easy in coming.

What could she tell her? That it wasn't her that was necessarily the problem? That it was Jude and the feelings Mary brought out in her?

No. She had to face this and deal with it. What a sweet, sweet problem it was, with Mary like the dancing flame of a fire. It lured her in with its warmth but could easily sting her with its burn. Despite the danger, it was wonderful, hypnotizing, drawing her closer.

She licked her lips and held the bottom of the chair.

Mary switched on the massager and put the head to her flesh. She was smooth there, having shaved since their first encounter, and Jude could see the seashell pink of her flesh and the redness of her clit as the massager moved around and around, stimulating just the edges.

"Mm," Mary said. "Feels so good." She jerked her hips a little and her face and neck crimsoned with desire. "I started touching myself, Jude. I realized I could do to myself what you did to me. I've been doing it every night. Making myself—"

She jerked wildly and her muscles tensed. Her hand stilled with the massager directly over her clit while her other hand released her flesh. The noise of the vibration changed as it pleasured her, nestling itself into her. She rocked back and forth while moaning, eyes closed, hand up in her hair and then on her face and down her neck.

Jude leaned forward, wanting to get closer, wanting to touch her.

Mary opened her eyes and found her. Then, with a grin so wicked and so erotic it nearly knocked Jude from her chair, she said, "Come." And she came loudly and throatily, body fucking the massager, her hand gripping and thrashing the sheets. Jude stood, her own pulse colliding with her hesitation. She wanted to tackle and take her, ravish her like there was no tomorrow.

But Mary climaxing was so intense and so beautiful, she didn't dare move. She watched, wishing she could capture the sight in a bottle to view and experience anytime she wanted.

Mary stilled. Her heavy and glossed-over eyes focused.

"Did you see me?" she asked. Her voice had that post orgasmic rasp to it and her face had that ease to it, as if the whole world and all its problems had just disappeared.

"I know you saw me," she said, confident, sexy. Fucking hot. "Here," she said, taking Jude's hand. "Feel." She placed it on her upper thigh where Jude could feel the beginning of her arousal.

Jude inhaled sharply and tried to move her hand further up.

"Oh, no," Mary said, laughing a little. "You're supposed to watch."

"I don't want to," Jude said, her voice tight with desire.

"No?"

"I want to touch you."

"You can't."

Jude stiffened. What? This was her room, her world, her rules.

Mary obviously saw the dismay on her face because she took her hand and brought it to her mouth. She dipped Jude's fingertips just inside and sucked. The sensation went directly to Jude's clit and she had the urge to touch herself and move her hips. She had to gently pull herself from Mary's mouth in order to keep what little control she had left.

"Don't get upset," Mary said, reaching out to touch her face.

"Upset is not the right word," Jude said. She didn't know what word would suffice, if any at all.

"I don't want you to have to do anything. I was wrong in expecting something from you. In wanting something more—"

Jude touched her lips to silence her. She couldn't stand hearing Mary blame herself for the feelings that coursed between them.

Mary kissed her fingers. "What you've given me, it's more than anyone else ever has."

"Don't thank me."

"I want to."

"I didn't do anything."

"Yes, you did. I know it probably didn't mean much to you—"

"Nein." Jude touched her mouth again. "Do not say that."

Mary moved her lips again, but Jude pressed firmer.

"Never say that."

Mary nodded and Jude slid her hand away.

"Will you watch me?" Mary asked.

Jude clenched her jaw and nodded. How could she possibly say no?

"Sit with me," Mary said, encouraging Jude to sit on her knees just as she was. "I need help with this one. Will you help me?"

Again, Jude nodded. Her skin was aflame with lust and she felt herself pool with wetness as Mary lubed up the small dildo and slid it into herself. She took Jude's hand and placed it on the flat base.

"Hold it inside me as I move," she said, switching on the massager once again. "I love this one. It feels so good. Makes me think of when you fucked me with one that first night. I saw stars. Millions and millions of—" Her breath hitched as she started to move.

"Jude," she said. "Look at me. Look at how good it feels."

She jerked her hips and Jude felt the shaft push against her hand. She groaned as she watched Mary gyrate into it, her surrounding flesh wet with shades of pink and red. The massager buzzed and Mary moaned, closing her eyes for long periods of time and then opening them to focus on Jude and move the massager closer to her clit.

"I always start off like this," she said, breathless. "I move the vibrator around and around, get myself all worked up, and then I give in to myself and hold it right here." She moved the head to her clit, dropped her other hand, and began to sway slowly. "See? Just like this." She bit her lower lip, the pleasure obviously mounting. "And it gets really good now. Really, really good. With the shaft and the ma—"

But Jude could take no more. She cupped Mary's jaw and dipped her head and kissed her, taking her sweet plump lips into her own, tasting and consuming. Mary seemed to melt right into her, so warm and limp and soft. Jude didn't give her time to protest, holding her tighter and pumping the cock in and out of her, slowly at first and then quicker. Mary reacted with a tight groan and a noisy intake of breath. And then, in an instant, she was clinging to her, kissing her deeply in return.

They melded, kissing and moaning, the vibrator buzzing and the cock fucking.

She came while Jude was in her mouth, her hand clawing at Jude's back while her entire body convulsed. Jude held her close and took in the way she felt against her, the way she smelled, the way she sounded. The way she absolutely loved to come.

Jude released Mary's lips to taste her cheek, her neck, and the thin sheen of sweat in the dip of her collarbone. It was like breaking open a coconut on a hot, sunny, waterless island, and she couldn't get enough of her. She licked and sucked and bit her just enough to get Mary to call out before stopping. Then she hurriedly tore open her shirt, loosened the knot, and tugged it from her arms.

Jude kissed her quickly each time she tried to speak. Next went her bra; the black lace was very sexy indeed, but Jude wanted no part of it and tossed it across the room. Mary's breasts were pert and moist with sweat, the nipples somewhere between firm and soft, and she made herself wait before taking them into her mouth.

"Lie down," Jude said, so close to her mouth she could sneak out her tongue for a taste. Their eyes locked and Jude saw exactly what Mary must be seeing in her. A want so intense no one else in the world could comprehend.

Mary eased back onto her behind, but she went no further.

"Make me," she said.

Jude hissed with dangerous desire and pressed her hand to Mary's sternum, forcing her to her back. Mary tried to come up, but Jude straddled her hips and held her down.

"You're going to have to hold me down," Mary said. "Did you hear me? I want you to hold me down while you take me."

Jude held her wrists like she'd done in her office. Held them tightly above her head. She kissed her again, long and deep and with more demand. Mary kissed her too, aggressively, trying to hold Jude's lips with her own. Her eager participation only made Jude hotter, and she rose, released her wrists, and tore off her own shirt.

"Yes," Mary said. "Fucking take it all off."

She tried to help Jude with her bra, but Jude pushed her away. "No."

"I want to see them," Mary said perched on her elbows. "Now."

Jude laughed a little, nervous but intrigued. "I have created a monster."

Mary only grinned that wicked grin, the one that would no doubt haunt Jude for days. "I can't help what I want."

Mary tried to touch her again, and Jude pinned her with one hand.

"I said no."

When she released her and straightened her back, Mary obeyed. She watched as Jude unlatched her bra and trailed it up her chest, then she tossed it aside and grabbed Mary's hands.

"You want to feel me?" Jude asked.

"Yes."

"How badly?"

"Very badly. So badly I've dreamt of it."

Jude placed Mary's warm hands on her breasts and they both breathed deeply. Jude leaned down and kissed her, slipping her tongue along her lips and then plunging deep inside. Mary groaned and squeezed her breasts, her thumbs grazing her awakening nipples. Jude bit Mary's lower lip softly in response and whispered in her ear.

"You dream about me, Mary?"

"Yes."

Jude closed her eyes and sat up. Mary's hands continued, her fingers playing across her nipples and caressing the underside of her breasts.

"I've dreamt of this," Mary said. "You on me like this. In my hands. Your face…"

Jude opened her eyes.

"Just like that," Mary said.

Jude began to rock against her, her own clit dangerously engorged and ready to burst.

"Have you dreamt of me?" Mary asked.

Jude stilled.

Mary stopped her hands and Jude saw a hint of panic in her eyes.

"You want to know?"

"Yes."

Jude leaned down. "You cannot know."

"But—"

Jude crawled from her and stood. She unfastened her pants and pulled them off along with her panties. She couldn't tell Mary the truth. That she did have dreams about her, almost every night. But what was more stirring was the encounter they were having now. It was like a fantasy, Mary literally the lover of her dreams. The things she said, the way she reacted, the way she wasn't afraid, and yet she was still so naïve.

She hurried to her dresser and retrieved her own cock, the one she used on no one else. It had been a while; she used it only when she could no longer resist the temptation to climax. Most never saw her insert it into herself, but tonight she wanted to use it and she wanted Mary to see.

Mary sat on the bed waiting and watching in silence. Jude appreciated her dropping the topic, and it allowed her to concentrate only on the moment. Mary was there to fuck and they both wanted it. She knew there was more, that there were growing feelings and something else that was wild and untamed, but it didn't matter. Nothing could stop her now. She had to have her.

She could only hope Mary meant what she said about wanting nothing more.

Jude returned to the bed and gently shoved Mary back down as she grinned.

"What's this?" she asked when Jude handed her the cock.

"Hold it." She grabbed the lube and squirted it onto the shaft. "Rub it on," she said, showing Mary how. As Mary worked the lube on, Jude retrieved Mary's small cock and readied it. Mary watched with wonder, her eyes full of excited curiosity. But she knew better than to ask questions.

"Now," Jude said, holding Mary's cock. "Spread your legs."

Mary obeyed and opened herself up. Jude traced her fingers along her wet thighs and purred.

"So wet, Mary." She rubbed her fingers in her slick folds and slid them easily into her opening. "And so ready." Mary tensed around her, and Jude was tempted to play with her some, but her own loins were demanding immediate attention. "Easy," Jude said, bringing the cock to her hole and slowly sliding it inside.

Mary held her breath and Jude went carefully, loving how tight she still was.

"Okay," Mary said and then visibly relaxed.

Jude pumped her a little and she nearly groaned as Mary gripped her arms and came up off the bed. She was ready.

Jude straddled her leg and instructed her softly. "Slide it inside me."

Mary didn't hesitate, bringing the cock to her at once. Jude angled it correctly and placed her hand over Mary's. She groaned heavily as it slid inside and filled her completely. Her hips began to sway and she stared down at Mary, loving the look she saw on her face. She bucked and groaned and licked her lips.

"You are fucking me, Mary. Yes, you are." She quickened her hips. "I am anchored to you." Her words were turning them both on and she touched Mary's heated cheek and bent to kiss her. Their tongues swirled and they both moaned, caught up in erotic bliss. Jude straightened and pumped Mary with her cock as she continued to ride hers.

"Feels so good," Mary said.

"Yes."

"Fucking. We are fucking."

"Yes."

"Oh God, we are fucking."

"Yes."

"You're riding me. Fucking my leg. You're so beautiful." She reached up, touched Jude's face, and trailed her fingers down to her tight abdomen. "So incredibly sexy." She touched her face again as her own melted with obvious pleasure.

"Jude."

"Yes."

"Jude."

"Yes."

"Oh God, Jude!"

"Yes, yes." Jude watched her face, her sweet, sweet face as she came. And then she clenched her eyes closed as her own orgasm overtook her, sending her hips into overdrive and her mind and heart into blood-pounding, pleasurable bliss. She'd never come like this before at Conquest. She'd never let herself go like this, fucking at the sheer mercy of another.

It had been a long time. A long, long time.

But God it was good. Insanely fucking wonderful.

And it was Mary. Mary Mary Mary.

"Ah." Her voice hitched as she rode out the last of it, her fingers intertwined with Mary's.

"Jude." Mary whispered her name as she stared at her with glossy eyes. Her body pushed the cock against Jude's hand as she eased it away. It caused Mary to sigh and her pelvis pumped once involuntarily.

"I feel full with fire all the way up, but…"

"But what?" Jude's voice gave away her rising emotion. She had to struggle not to look away.

"I feel empty without you in me."

Jude cleared her throat and shifted, swinging herself off the cock and off Mary. She sat at the edge of the bed and tried to get control of herself. She didn't know why her sudden emotions surprised her. She was the one who'd allowed this to happen. She was the one who'd told Mary to slide the cock up in her and fuck her. She was the one who'd looked into her eyes and come with her.

Fuck.

She held her head in her hands for a few seconds before she realized she was doing it. She stood as Mary noticed.

"Are you okay?"

"Yes."

"Did you enjoy that?"

She busied herself cleaning the cock and putting it away. As she closed the dresser drawer she answered. "Yes." She heard Mary take in a deep breath.

"I did too. More than I can say or should say."

"Then don't."

There was silence. Jude couldn't yet face her. She knew the look she'd see in Mary's eyes, and it would penetrate her already failing defenses just like it always did.

"Okay. I won't."

More silence. Jude stood very still, running her fingertips in a repeating circular pattern along the dresser top. She didn't know what to say. Didn't trust herself to say anything. She'd come with her. Collided with her on a mental plane of monumental meaning and emotion. And even though she was doing her damndest to hide it, her insides could tell no lies. They were thrumming and sizzling and melting into one another in a dance of freedom and new connections. A part of her wanted to scream in revelation while another part of her wanted to run far and fast, never to experience such feelings again.

"Jude?"

This was it. A decision was going to be placed before her. The gauntlet was going to come down along with the guillotine and slice this in two. Which side would she take?

"Yes?"

"Do you want me to leave now?"

The cut was quick and precise. Two halves fell open and stared up at her. The decision came, riding cloaked and hidden among her emotions. It voiced itself before her rational and fearful side could defend itself.

"No."

Mary exhaled in obvious relief, but she seemed to sense Jude's continued guarded mood.

"Can I touch you?"

"No."

"With my mouth?"

"No."

More silence.

"What would you like to do then?"

Jude fought trembling as she breathed deeply. The answer came quickly again though she didn't know where from.

"I want to make you come again. With my mouth."

"Do you want to do that as badly as I want to do it to you?"

"Yes."

"How can you be sure?"

Jude turned, the fiery desire she had for Mary returning in an instant, heating and beating beneath her skin. "Because I have tasted you. I have felt your flesh swell and tremble in my mouth. I have swallowed the hot slickness of your desire as it pulsed out of you. I have had it. I have had you. And I want it again."

Mary blinked rapidly as if the words were so heavy and powerful she couldn't quite allow them entry all at once. When they did seem to sink in, she had the look of a woman fulfilled and yet hungry for more. She moved eagerly to the foot of the bed where she stacked the pillows behind her back.

"Come here," she said. "Sit." She pointed to the floor. "On your knees."

Jude didn't move, the loss of control messing with her head again.

"Why?"

"Do it and find out." Mary scooted to the edge of the bed and spread her legs. She looked at Jude expectantly and trailed her fingertips along her wet flesh, carefully avoiding her most sensitive spot.

Jude found herself moving, falling to her knees. It was defeat at its sweetest and most rewarding. She groaned at the pain of it as well as at the heaven that lay before her.

"There," Mary said leaning back a little. She was propped up on the pillows and still able to see Jude. Her fingers sank deeper into her folds and began circling her clit.

"Do you want to touch it?" she breathed. "Because, God, I want you to."

Jude closed her eyes as they rolled back in erotic expectation. She tried like hell to get control, to make herself say no and walk away. This path was dangerous with caution signs everywhere. But just imagining Mary's flesh in her mouth caused her to lick her lips and carry on. When she opened her eyes and saw Mary's fingers massaging ever quicker and closer, she knew she was doomed.

"Lick me," Mary said, her breath hitching in her chest.

Jude leaned forward and snaked out her tongue.

"Lick me while I touch myself."

Another groan of mad desire escaped Jude as she pressed her tongue to her. Mary jerked and hissed as Jude's tongue found her peeking flesh between her moving fingers. She laughed in gluttonous delight as Jude pushed firmer, licking her fingers and her flesh all at once.

"Yes, baby. That's so good. Do you like it? Do you like the way I feel?"

"Yes."

"Is this what you wanted?"

"Yes." But she couldn't get enough. She needed more. The teasing bits of pink flesh weren't nearly enough and she knew

Mary felt the same way. She could tell by her breathing and the way she tensed with wanton need each time she stopped. "Move your hand," Jude said huskily trying to move her by the wrist.

Mary laughed. "Not yet."

Jude inched closer and used more of her weight as she leaned into her and licked. Mary thrashed a little, moaning and panting. She gyrated her hand, moving her flesh as Jude licked. She was loving it, teasing herself as well as Jude.

"I need more," she finally said. Her eyes flashed at Jude and they both stilled.

She held herself open, beckoning. "Lick me. Please."

Jude felt her mouth water and she fell into her quickly, saturating her flesh with her mouth.

"Oh, fuck!" Mary cried, knotting her fingers in Jude's hair. "Yes!"

Jude licked heavily and then sucked, licked heavily, and then sucked. She consumed her like a woman dying, taking her in as if she were life force herself.

Mary went insane with pleasure, her abdomen tensing as she watched and took. Her fingers played Jude's scalp as she spoke in broken pieces.

"Yes. Oh God, Jude. Fuck. Oh fuck! I love it. I love it. I love it so fucking much. I'm going to—I'm so close. Oh God!"

Jude was sure Mary was going over and she was close to doing the same. But Mary spoke suddenly and loudly.

"Stop!"

Jude froze. Mary gasped and pushed her away. Jude had to swallow a few times before she could speak.

"Ah, fuck I was so close. So close." She sat up completely and took Jude's face in her hands. "It was so good."

Jude wanted to ask her why she stopped, but she didn't speak. She didn't want to sound needy. It wasn't in her to do so. But she couldn't stop her insides from screaming with want. She wanted to finish her off like she was the feast of a lifetime. She wanted to make Mary come so hard she screamed and begged and cried for a mercy she didn't really want.

"You want more, don't you?" Mary asked, stroking her cheek. Jude stood, unable to take the teasing of her touch.

"You don't have to say it. I can see it in your eyes. Those wickedly beautiful eyes."

Jude tried not to look at her, but she was so beautiful and hungry with tinted cheeks and swollen lips. Her chest heaved with her breathing, her pert breasts eager and reaching up for more. And the stockings. Jude wanted to remove them only to lick where every web of fabric had touched.

"I told you what I want," Jude replied.

"You want to make me come."

"Yes."

"Come back for more then."

Jude clenched her jaw and stared as Mary began touching herself again.

Jude licked her lips to taste another sample of her. It only made her hungrier.

"No." Jude steeled herself. The teasing would continue, she was sure of it. The game was far from over, and as much as it intrigued and excited her, the journey itself was torturous.

This is what it feels like to not have control. This is what it feels like to want someone so fucking badly...

"No?" Mary stood and approached. She ran her hand up Jude's core to between her breasts. Jude caught her by the wrist.

"I have another hand," she said, the corner of her mouth lifting with devilish intent.

Jude gripped her other wrist and they faced off with a tense stare.

"I have a mouth, Jude." She stood on her toes and kissed her lips. "And a body." She rubbed herself against Jude.

Jude shuddered. The feel of her was intoxicating, the scent of her damp skin and heated scalp going straight to her center.

"You can't stop me, Jude. Not forever."

"Yes, I can." She held her tightly but didn't turn away from her soft kiss when it came again. How easy it would be to just close her eyes and get lost in it. How easy. And how utterly terrifying.

"No, you can't, Jude. Know why? Because you don't really want to." She leaned in and licked Jude's neck. Jude pushed her away, but Mary, unwilling to go, grabbed Jude in return and tightened her fingers around her forearms.

"You want me. Just as badly as I want you."

"Let me go." But Mary wasn't threatened and Jude knew her voice reflected her doubt. Even though Mary was plucking deep, buried chords of emotion in her, she was also turning her on.

"Take me," Mary said, trying to nibble her lip. "Fucking take me like I know you want to."

"And if I don't?" Would this insanity end? Maybe for the moment. But the empty night and empty days following would be more than harrowing. To have her was suicide. To resist her certain madness.

"I don't know. You tell me."

She knew. She fucking knew. She could obviously read Jude like an open book.

"You need to leave." Her stomach knotted and flipped. But she didn't really want her to go. Not yet. Not until she had her every which way from Sunday.

Mary laughed. "Okay then." She released Jude and stepped away. Jude watched as she reached across the bed to retrieve her toys. A sheen of sweat ran down the center of her back and Jude yearned to lick it, imagining Mary turned and riding her cock, hips thrusting, back glistening.

"It was fun, wasn't it?" Mary asked, placing her cocks and massager in her purse. "We didn't even get to the big phallus though. That's too bad. I really wanted to try that with you. God, I can already imagine it filling me up with that forceful heat." She shook her head and continued packing. "Maybe next time."

"Why are you doing this?" Jude asked, unable to move. All she could do was watch helplessly.

Mary was buttoning up her shirt. "What do you mean? Doing what?"

"You know what I mean, Mary."

She paused. "I'm not doing anything, Jude. I'm only playing by your rules. I'm only playing your game. Only…" She walked up to her and placed a finger on her lips. Jude resisted the urge to take the finger into her mouth and suck it, as if it had been dipped in rich, dark honey. "I'm the one in control. I don't think you like that very much do you?"

Jude felt herself flush and it angered her. Why was Mary so good at getting to her? And why couldn't Jude move? Why was she nailed to the spot allowing all this to go on around her?

"Then again, I know you like it just fine." Mary took advantage of her stilled position and took her hand. She sank it between the cool, slick folds of her flesh. "I sure do." She moved it back and forth and kicked her hips into it. "Yeah. Oh, yeah." When Jude responded with the movement of her fingers, Mary rose onto her toes and whispered in her ear. "But you can't make me come anymore." She kept moving, rocking into her. "Don't you want to know why?"

Jude swallowed but didn't speak. Her fingers were caught up in a web of arousal. It would be so easy to just shove herself deep inside her. Throw her back against the wall and fuck her madly, biting into her neck and shoulder as she came. It would be so easy…

Mary was watching her closely as if she could see into her mind. She stopped moving and removed Jude's hand. "Because you won't let me touch you."

Jude suddenly found her feet and she took a step back, her brain not registering the meaning of the words as quickly as it should. Mary continued."You know how badly you want to touch me, lick me, make me come? Well, that's how badly I want to do it to you."

"You—"

"Yes, I do. Now you know what it feels like to not be able to. To not be able to do what you want, what you most desire." Her face was set and serious. There was no more flirting or playful seductive banter. "Don't say anything. It's not needed. I know that for whatever reason, you won't let me. That's okay. I understand as I hope you now do." She walked back to her bag and finished dressing.

Jude was at a total loss for words. When she did manage to start speaking, Mary was quick to stop her. She left her with some last words as she breezed past her to the door.

"If you want to play again, you know where to find me. But from now on, we play by my rules."

CHAPTER TWELVE

I'm crazy. I'm totally fucking crazy." Mary gripped her steering wheel and shook it, trying to pry it from the column. She'd just had the most powerful and sexually charged night of her life. She'd done it. She'd gone in there and taken control, making Jude do what she wanted. It was clearly insane behavior, completely out of her league, but it had worked. Jude had touched her, wanted her. She'd even come with her.

Oh my God!

She eased down her window and screamed. "I'm fucking crazy!"

She laughed as the wind whipped her hair and teased her ear. God, she felt good. The new attitude was working wonders and now that she'd gotten what she wanted…

She slowed for a red light and checked herself in the rearview mirror. Her eyes were dark with liner and mascara. They were sexy but stirring with things she didn't understand.

She'd had her fun and had gotten her way. Well, not totally, but still, for the most part.

What about Jude?

She accelerated roughly as the light changed. Jude would be fine, despite the lost look on her face as she'd left. Jude was good at the game. The master. She could handle it.

Yeah, but can I?

She pressed her lips together and nodded. She could. She was ready. Bring it on. Hopefully, Jude would come knocking, but if she didn't, that was okay too. She knew what mind-blowing sex was now, and she could either give it to herself or find it on her own.

The thought scared her a little. Could she really be like Jude and approach women with confidence and an air of expected respect? More than that, could she actually find someone she was attracted to like she was Jude? She laughed nervously and the wind blew it back at her. She didn't like the way it felt, and she eased up her window and wrung her hands on the steering wheel the rest of the way home.

After parking in her garage and closing the door, she went to her phone and checked her voice mail. A small part of her, bigger than she wanted to admit, thought there might actually be a message from Jude begging her for more, wanting to come over. But she had no messages and her cell phone had been silent. She pushed away the disappointment already starting to try to surface.

"I need a drink." She kicked off her heels and rolled off her stockings. Her legs tingled a little at the feel of fresh air as she strode through her small kitchen to the cabinet next to the fridge. She pulled down an old bottle of Scotch and downed a shot straight from the lip. She winced a little and screwed on the cap, hoping the big sip would be enough to relax her.

Sighing, she leaned against the countertop and absorbed the calm silence of her kitchen. The pale yellow walls soothed her, but the quiet of her cozy home was starting to bother her. Her old routine of coming home, making a small, easy dinner, and sitting in front of the television all night had been cast aside days ago. She rarely bothered with dinner now, and the television offered nothing to compete with Jude Jaeger. Her evenings were spent doing homework, pacing the living room as she went over all the different ways she could see Jude, calling the club and hanging up, and then going to her room to bring herself to climax countless times until sleep finally claimed her.

She'd hoped after her earlier success in seeing Jude, that the night would bring some much needed comfort and peace. But the normally tranquil walls of her home still seemed gaping and empty, silently mocking her.

She thought back to the harsh words spoken by her co-workers about how she probably lived alone with twenty-five cats. She didn't even have a cat, or any other pet, and instead of that comforting her, it just sounded all the more pathetic. What had she done with the last ten years?

She'd hidden away in her little house hoping and praying the rest of the world would just leave her alone.

Alone.

She was definitely alone. She pushed off the counter and headed straight to her bedroom. She flicked on the light and stripped. The shower called to her, but she decided against it. Instead, she crawled into bed and held her blouse close to her face. The smell of Jude's cologne rocketed through her and she shivered with desire, her nipples hardening and her clit pulsing.

How badly she wanted Jude in her bed. Every night. Every single night.

How long would this yearning last? Was there ever a cure? What if Jude wasn't enough?

She thought back to their heated time together and her hand drifted to between her legs. They'd come together, and she knew she'd never forget the look in Jude's eyes as ecstasy had overcome her. As the memory of it floated though her mind, she opened her legs and stroked her clitoris. Her flesh was still painfully swollen and it didn't take long to bring herself to the brink of desire. The climax was powerful but quick, and she kept stroking with Jude's face in her mind. She came again loudly, arching her back off the bed. Yes, yes, yes. Oh God.

Jude's face still hovered as she sank into the sheets. It watched over her and spoke softly, wishing her a good night. She nestled into her blouse and breathed deeply.

Would anything ever be enough again? Mary didn't know. And as she closed her eyes and breathed in Jude's scent, she was sure of just one thing.

Whether she could get enough of Jude or not, nothing would ever be the same.

CHAPTER THIRTEEN

Jude drove past the beautiful looming mountain she usually hiked after work. The dusty trail wound up and around the side promising a spectacular desert view from the top. But today, even if she skipped walking it to run, she knew it wouldn't be enough of a workout to kill the thrumming inside. Work had done nothing to help either, and she'd left a bit early before Mary's class let out just so she wouldn't risk running into her.

She knew if she had seen her she would've caved and slid to her like a magnet moving toward steel. She would've spoken to her, said things she'd dreamt about the night before. "Come with me. I want to touch you again. Let me take you, Mary." And they would've ended up in her office again, tearing at each other like bloodthirsty tigers. And there was also the threat of the tease. The new rules Mary had come up with, promising Jude only some of the pie while waving the rest right in her face.

She'd hated it almost as much as it turned her on, which only made her hate it more.

Mary lying there on the edge of the bed, stocking-covered legs splayed, hand massaging her folds, telling Jude to lick her, lick her through her fingers.

Goddamn sexy woman. An ingénue coming into her own, boldly casting aside her innocence and naivety to get what she wanted. Jude had to respect her for that, even though she knew she was the ultimate target. Mary wanted her and wanted to touch her. And it didn't seem like she was going to give up anytime soon. Jude had to come up with a way to resist her or a way to take back control. At the moment, she could think of neither, and total avoidance was impossible because Mary knew where to find her.

She pulled into a parking space and killed the engine to her BMW.

She didn't want to totally avoid Mary.

"Fuck." She palmed her forehead. That was the truth of it. The other truth of it was just as devastating and confusing and terribly frightening.

She wanted Mary to touch her.

She climbed from the car with her duffel bag in hand. The building before her was old and nondescript. If it had been painted black and located in a more populated area, it would've reminded her of Conquest. But its faded yellow paint and blowing dust surroundings countered that image. A small bell over the door jingled as she pushed her way inside. Immediately, the bell sound was stifled by the sound of repeated thumping and male voices yelling instruction. She hadn't been to a boxing gym in years, and the smells of sweat, old mats, and dozens of used wraps and gloves reminded her of times long ago. Memories tried to flood her, but she forced them away, needing the more pressing reason for her visit to stay in mind.

She had come to work. To work hard.

As she moved further inside, she ignored a few stunned and curious glances and made her way toward the back to the locker room. The smell inside rose in strength from that of the open floor, and she was relieved to find a separate door marked "Women." The area was smaller than the main gym, but it looked and smelled cleaner. A wedge of six lockers, which had obviously been removed from a larger bay, sat against the wall along with a single bench and two good-sized bathroom stalls. A small row of three sinks sat across from the stalls.

After finding a locker and changing her clothes, she put away her duffel bag, closed the locker, and headed out. She tucked her gloves under her arm and welcomed what little heated breeze there was to the bare skin of her arms and midsection as she stepped once again into the main gym. More glances came, sizing up her tight-fitting sports bra and basketball shorts. She let them stare, focusing instead on dropping her gloves to shake out her limbs and stretch. As she worked on her hamstring, she wondered who she needed to ask to borrow some tape. It had been years since she'd boxed, and she needed to give her hands and wrists all the support they would need in order for her to aggressively attack the bags.

She found what appeared to be a makeshift office nestled between storage rooms and she crossed to it after a series of long and effective stretches. The crowded gym pulsed around her, and despite the gym's three window air conditioners, the place felt heavy with expelled carbon dioxide and moist heat.

More glances fell upon her as she walked. Men were everywhere, half naked, greased up like holiday turkeys, dodging and jabbing and grunting. One of them, a rare one who was still clothed, trotted up to her as she was waiting by the door to the office.

"You are my girl?" he asked smiling. "You are big. I was worried you would be too small."

She stared at him, completely confused. He had on a dark green T-shirt and matching striped athletic pants. The gym's logo was written in white across his chest.

"You are late. I hope you are warm." He appeared to be Hispanic with dark hair and deeply tanned skin. His accent was strong, but he was easily understood. He took her gloves, which weren't professional or standard, and tossed them aside. Next, he grabbed her hands and began a deep massage with his rough but strong fingers.

She started to pull away, but he seemed intent, knowing something she didn't.

"I don't understand," she finally said.

He released her hands to dig in his pocket and retrieve a roll of white tape. She watched in surprised silence as he quickly and expertly taped up her hands, winding between her fingers and covering up through her wrists.

"Nothing to understand. She is ready." He looked at her shoes and scoffed. "What is this?"

"Nikes," she said, growing frustrated. "She? Who is she?"

"No, no, no." He walked away and gestured for her to follow. They were headed for the far ring where Jude saw something that made her stop in her tracks. In the ring's corner stood a tall woman with long dark hair pulled back into a ponytail. Her black sports bra showed every impossibly hard muscle from her chiseled broad shoulders down to her long, powerful legs. She held Jude's gaze as a short man next to her continued to rub her arms.

Jude set her jaw and composed herself.

"Come on," her man in green said, waving her over. They stood together outside the ropes. He examined Jude's hands and then knocked her off balance as he lifted her foot. She caught a rope and cursed. But before she could say more, he removed her shoe and trotted around the ring to the woman's corner. Jude watched as the three conversed. The woman nodded and pointed with her glove-covered hands. She turned back around and hopped quickly in place, dark eyes fastened to Jude. And then, ever so quickly and sneakily, she smirked.

The man hurried up to Jude with boxing gloves and ring shoes.

"Aqui," he said and handed over the shoes.

Anger swept through Jude as she realized what was about to happen. The man wanted her to box with this woman. And he wanted her to wear her shoes and gloves in doing so.

"No," Jude said. She came here to work, to hit, to sweat. To fucking erase her world for a while. Not to battle with a stranger.

The man seemed confused but pressed on. "Your size." He showed her the shoes and bent as if he were about to put them on.

"No."

The man froze. "No?"

"No."

He rose and shouted something about zapatos across the ring. The woman crossed to them, resting her forearms on the rope as she looked down at Jude.

"What's the problem?"

Jude felt herself inhale deeply to stand taller. "I don't want this," she said.

"Why not?" The woman's eyes were deep but not endless.

"I don't have to explain."

"I think you do." Her gaze fell to Jude's breasts and then slowly came back up.

"No, I do not."

"First you're late, and now you're chicken?"

Jude nearly shook with growing anger. "You are mistaken."

The woman pushed off from the ropes. "I don't think so." She smirked again as if she'd won the match ten times over. Then her face hardened. "Get lost. You're wasting everyone's time."

Jude had to turn away. What was happening was impossible, inconceivable. Jude hadn't thought specifically of her ex in a long, long time. Not even when Mary brought about rising and growing emotion did she think of her. Her emotions for Mary were scary, yes, and they reminded her of how she once felt, but never had she let Nicole cross her mind. But here she was in a gym in the middle of nowhere with a woman who in no way resembled her first and last love. But her demeanor, her confident and cocky presence, and the words coming out of her mouth were just like her.

Get lost, Jude.

Don't waste my time with all this love bullshit.

What is wrong with you?

Grow up and grow a spine.

It was fun while it lasted.

No. No. She tried to shake it away. This wasn't why she'd come here. But admittedly, the last time she'd come was soon after the breakup. She should've known better, should've foreseen the emotional link.

I can control it.

She forced herself to breathe. Her body took in the oxygen eagerly and began to calm, but her mind raced with thoughts and images from long ago. Laughter from across the ring caught her attention and she turned to find the woman and the short man next to her laughing. They were looking at Jude and snickering. They had obviously confused her with someone else and they wanted her to fight. Logic told her to let them laugh as she walked away. But pride and long ago wounds demanded that she stay and give them what they wanted.

Jude snatched up the shoes and sat to put them on. She pulled the laces so hard and tight she thought for sure they'd snap. The man in green was suddenly by her side again and helping her on with her gloves.

"She is fast," he said. "Strong as un toro. Very strong. She has chin like iron and uppercut like God himself." He patted her gloves and massaged her muscles. "Move. Move, move, move. If you get hit, back away and she will stop. She will go easy with you." He held her face and then slipped on padded headgear. Then he pointed at her mouth and frowned. She needed a mouth guard. He ran into one of the storage rooms. Jude took the opportunity to climb into the ring. The woman was staring her down as they both jogged in place and threw jabs and crosses. Jude made sure not to look away from her, even when the man returned with a fresh mouth guard. After he slipped it in he gave her more instructions, but she couldn't understand all of it. She wasn't fluent in Spanish. She considered questioning him, but it was damn near impossible with the mouth guard. And when the woman smirked again, Jude didn't care at all about what he may have said.

She charged into the center of the ring and waved the woman over. The woman threw her head back and laughed and then came forward. The men started flinging Spanish slurs and instructions right away as Jude stood there with her arms at her side. She smiled and the woman threw a quick jab. Jude dodged it and the next one and they began to dance around the ring. She knew the woman was testing her distance, and the second she got it right, Jude would have to step it up.

The woman threw a few more, careful not to leave herself open. Jude managed to bob and weave around them, keeping her feet as light as she could. Her plan was simple. Keep the woman punching and wear her out. She was big and strong and made of iron, and gassing her out was her safest option.

With every empty jab she threw, Jude could see the frustration building in her eyes. The man in green was screaming at Jude to put her hands up, but she ignored him, preferring to dance naked with the devil. She had a point to prove, not only to the woman, but to herself, and it wasn't happening quickly enough. So she stopped her movement and waved the woman over again. More screaming came from the man in green, and the woman had a brief look of confusion. The next second a hard cross connected with Jude's chin, snapping her head back and to the side. She felt her jaw give, like a disk slipping quickly out of place, and the pain shot up through her head and into her scalp. She stumbled backward and pressed her gloves to her temples, trying to get her eyeballs back into place.

Blinking, she refocused on the woman, who stood wearing that same damn smirk. Jude opened and closed her mouth, testing her jaw, pushing on it with her glove. She wasn't badly hurt. The cross had been hard and unexpected. She'd been waiting for another jab. The woman was smart and merciless. Jude bounced on her toes and stepped in once more. The woman was still grinning at her as Jude threw out a couple of her own quick jabs. None of them connected and she concentrated more on her feet. She knew she was throwing her punches too quickly in regard to her forward step. She had to wait just a little more before she jabbed. She inched closer and closer. The woman was dodging her, not bothering to punch at Jude. Jude stepped closer and threw a bait jab. The woman fell for it by dodging and countering with a hook to Jude's body.

Jude blocked it with her left arm and then powered back with her own hook. It landed on the woman's lower jaw and neck, stunning her for the briefest of seconds. As hard as the punch was, it failed to move her, and before Jude knew it, the woman was stepping into her, throwing crosses, mixing in quick jabs, and connecting on several shots to her body. She was pounding Jude backward, her punches too random-feeling and quick. The man in green had been right. The woman was strong and fast. Too much for Jude. But she kept on going, no holds barred. The men were still yelling, wanting her to stop, but the woman waved them off, telling them no. She wanted to continue and she danced around Jude's punches gracefully, only taking one of the jabs to her temple. It seemed to piss her off and she came at Jude hard, throwing more combinations. Jude dodged as many as she could, trying to get the woman to chase her around the ring. Then she countered with her own assault, but as gassed as the woman was, she was still able to block Jude's throws.

Jude put all she had into each punch, convinced she must land at least one. But when one half connected, the woman came back harder than ever, hitting Jude in the nose, right jaw again, and along her torso. Stumbling, Jude found herself against the ropes, her face on fire, her lungs burning. She staggered then tried to walk back out to face off again.

She wouldn't quit. She wasn't a quitter. She had to hit her. Harder, faster. Had to kill the voice of the past. But hands and arms were suddenly on her shoulders, forcing her back to the corner. The man in green was removing her headgear and mouth guard. He looked frantic and angry, nimble fingers examining her face. She winced as a large Q-tip was shoved into her nose.

"What did you do? Are you crazy?" He rattled off in Spanish and she held her hands up over her head and was eventually able to catch her breath.

"I fought," she said, watching him remove her boxing gloves.

"You fought!" He shook his head. "You were not supposed to. Not like that. What is wrong with you?"

She licked her swollen lip and took the towel he offered to wipe her face and forehead. Her face was sore but not awful. Her nose throbbed, but by some miracle it wasn't bleeding. Her teeth and jaw ached and there was a painful stitch in her side, but she felt better than she had before. Her adrenaline was flowing and her body was going from numb to heavy with fatigue.

He tossed the gloves aside and cut away the tape from her hands. She flexed them and knew they'd be sore later.

"You can't do this again," he said. "I can't put my fighter in danger."

She laughed. "I wasn't in any danger. Besides, she wanted it." Jude looked at her across the way. She was leaning back against her corner ropes as her man cut her hand tape and checked her face and body. She was still watching Jude with the same deadly but curious eyes.

They had both wanted it. And now that she thought about it, in some ways it had been a bit…sexual. The dance, the opening and closing distance, the looks, it had all been like some sort of foreplay. And despite her fatigue and battle weary body, she was stirred, needing to battle the woman in another way.

She pushed away from the corner and slipped between the ropes.

The man in green tried to follow her. "Next time—"

"There will not be a next time," she said, heading toward the locker room. She entered and went straight to the sinks. Her face wasn't as red as she had expected it to be and the only sign of a fight she could see was her slightly swollen lip and the Q-tip, which she removed and tossed into the garbage. She rinsed her face and hair and shook the cold water away. She gasped as it ran down into her bra.

"Who are you?" a voice came from behind.

Jude saw the woman in the mirror and turned. "No one."

"You aren't my sparring partner, are you?"

"No."

"I didn't think so."

"What gave me away?"

The woman laughed. "Too many to list."

Jude walked toward her. "I thought I did pretty well."

The towel the woman held fell from her hand. "You did. For a novice."

Jude stood inches from her, facing off once again. The woman had her beat in height and strength. That was unusual.

"It was brave of you to fight." The smirk reappeared. "And very, very stupid."

"That is what you think."

"How could I think anything else?"

"You don't know me. You don't know that I got exactly what I wanted. Well…" She focused on the woman's full maroon lips. "Almost."

The woman again moved quickly, this time cupping Jude's face and pulling it toward her for a forceful, hot kiss. Jude knotted her fingers in her hair, holding her tightly as their tongues came slick and serious, searching for dominance. Wet skin on skin slid as they locked together and devoured each other. Jude tried to walk her back to the wall, but the woman was stronger and she resisted and pushed, leading Jude back into one of the larger stalls. The woman tore away from her long enough to close the door and secure it. When she came at Jude again she didn't speak, just gripped Jude's bra and yanked it up over her head, tangling it around her wrists. Then, holding her hands up like that, the woman attacked her breasts with a hungry, hot mouth, slipping Jude's nipples inside with an eager tongue, sucking so hard Jude almost fell to her knees.

Fighting the sensation, Jude pushed back, sidestepped, and was able to free her arms. But her hands were still tangled and the woman took advantage, lowering herself to attach to Jude's center through her shorts. She was digging with her fingers, pulling Jude's shorts aside, trying to sneak her tongue in on her bare flesh.

Jude squeezed her eyes closed, the feeling wonderful and terrifying, and she shoved on the woman's head, trying desperately to get her to stop. But the woman kept on, relentless, leaving Jude no other choice. She had to stop; she didn't let anyone touch her without permission—oh God, the tongue hit her, lips kissing her, mouth trying to latch on. She pushed her again and grew frantic. She wasn't in control. Somehow, she managed to free her hands and, with palms on the woman's shoulders, Jude shoved her away, knocking her back and off-balance.

Jude rushed her, pinned her against the wall, and bit into her neck as she drove her hand down the front of her pants. She found her clit soaked with arousal and she went right for the kill, thrusting her fingers deep inside. The woman threw her head back and groaned, her hands pulling and pinching Jude's nipples. Jude wanted to fend her off but she couldn't risk trying. And what she was doing, the aggressive way in which she was attacking her nipples, it was only arousing her further.

"You're a hot little thing," the woman said.

"Don't talk," Jude said, pumping her harder.

The woman held her tightly, laughing and kissing on Jude's shoulder. "But you're not as strong as me."

Jude added another finger and used her thumb to flick her clit. She had to keep control, keep the woman against the wall and in her hand.

"Agh, yeah, you're good. Really good. I like you."

The statement burned in Jude's ears.

I like you, Jude. What's the problem?

"Don't."

"Don't what?" The woman again played with Jude's breasts.

"Talk."

She grinned. "Okay."

But they began to battle again, the woman trying to push her away. Jude fought her, fucking her with one hand while the other pushed up on her sports bra. She fed from her quickly, sucking as hard as she could on her nipple while she pumped her. The woman's groans grew longer and louder, her hips began to buck.

Her fingers knotted in Jude's hair as she hissed her pleasure in heated whispers.

"Yeah. That's it. Hot little thing."

Jude fucked her with all her might, facing off with her past. Nicole used to do her just like this, taking her up against the wall, getting her off, making her come all over herself. Then she'd laugh and tease her, deciding whether or not she could touch her.

What can I say, babe, you're a hot fuck. I love doing you.

The woman began to move faster. Her groaning stopped, along with her whispers. Jude bit her nipple and it sent her over.

"Agh! Agh, yeah!"

She battled Jude with her hips and hole, pushing and constricting. And before the orgasm was over, she attacked Jude again, forcing her back to the other wall. She continued to ride Jude's hand as she looked down at her.

"Yeah, mmm, that's it. You're good aren't you. You know you are." Laughter came from her and she finally stopped and removed Jude's hand.

"You got me so wet."

She was a striking woman, standing there tall and dark and handsome. Her body was like a Greek statue of perfection, and she was as passionate about sex as she was fighting.

But Jude had had enough.

The woman was oblivious, though, and started to kneel. "My turn."

"No." Jude held her face and the woman stood.

"Come on. You can't tease me anymore. It isn't fair."

"I'm not teasing. I need to go."

The woman leaned into her and stroked her flesh through her shorts.

"You're soaking. I can feel it. You can't tell me you don't want it."

Jude closed her eyes at her use of another familiar phrase.

She held her wrist just like she'd done Mary's.

Mary.

It was like a breath of heaven and warmth and pleasure tenfold.

"I don't."

The woman stilled.

"What?"

Jude stepped by her and retrieved her bra. She opened the stall door and spoke. "Thanks for the dance." She walked to the bench, tugged on her bra, and removed her shoes. She left them there, retrieved her duffel bag, and walked into the main gym. She found her Nikes and slipped them on and saw the man in green talking to another tall, well-built woman. The real sparring partner must've arrived. He started to come toward her, but the hard look on her face must've stopped him.

The mild night air greeted her as she exited, leaving the gym behind for good. She felt better in some ways and worse in others. As she drove home she thought about the woman and their powerful encounter. But another woman returned to mind as she continued to drive home.

The woman she still couldn't seem to get from her mind.

Mary.

CHAPTER FOURTEEN

Mary couldn't concentrate and sat doodling at her desk, wishing her phone would ring to give her something to do. The office was somewhat quiet with those around her having a slow day too. She wanted to call Jude, had even looked up the phone number to her office at the college, but she decided against it. She had to leave her alone. At least for a while.

She'd seen her the evening before as she'd arrived early for class. Jude had been leaving, walking quickly to her vehicle. Mary had hid nearby, watching her curiously. Jude had seemed stiff, her piercing eyes hidden by sunglasses. Her gait was purposeful and her mouth set. She'd crawled into her BMW and driven away hurriedly.

Mary had wondered with a sinking stomach, whom she was going to see. A date? Someone at Conquest? How many would she have that night?

She rose and crossed the office to the break room. She needed a drink to help settle her once again churning stomach. She needed to release Jude from the dungeon of her tortured mind. Mary knew it and had been busy trying, but it hadn't happened.

Carla Meeker nearly bumped into her as she opened the break room door.

"Mary, hi." She looked her up and down quickly and Mary fought her old instinct to look away and slump into herself and instead pulled her shoulders back to stand taller.

"You look great."

Mary held her gaze. "Thank you." She thought about returning the compliment but didn't. Carla, in her opinion, looked like a high-priced hooker. Which probably was exactly the look she was going for.

"Seriously, I love the colors you've added to your wardrobe."

Really? Great. Maybe she should go back to her grays and browns.

Mary smiled and then when Carla didn't speak, she shouldered past her.

"I still want to get together, Mary," she said after her.

"Okay," Mary responded, not bothering to turn back. She heard the door close and she fished for coins in her slacks pockets, anxious for a diet soda.

"It's Mary, right?"

Mary turned and found another co-worker in the corner, flipping through a magazine. It was one of the women she'd heard talking about her that day in the bathroom.

"Does it matter?" Her heart began to twitch quicker as she thought about it. The machine kicked out her drink and she cracked the top and sipped hurriedly so as not to say anything she might regret.

"I'm Bethany."

Mary nodded.

"I heard what Carla said and she's right. You look really nice." Her smile was sincere and her words soft. Mary looked at her for a long moment and decided to be honest.

"Really? You mean I no longer look like a Bible salesman?"

Bethany's face went blank and then reddened as she remembered. "You heard—"

"I've heard a lot of the things that have been said about me around here."

"I'm so sorry. People are—can be—"

"Terrible?"

She nodded.

"It seems to be in the water around here."

"Yes, it does."

Mary studied her and recalled that Bethany had been the more mellow of the two, having said little in the way of harm in regard to her. Maybe she wasn't so bad. She came off as kind of nice.

"I'm afraid I've allowed myself to get caught up in it a few times."

"Yes, you have," Mary surprised herself in saying.

"I have?"

She took another long sip of her soda and joined Bethany at the small table. "I heard you one day. In the ladies' room."

"Oh." Her blush deepened. "I was afraid that might've been the case." She raised a nervous hand to twirl her chin length chestnut brown hair. Her eyes were a pale blue, the kind that seemed to glisten with bits of white. "I'm sorry," she said softly. She stood and Mary saw her hands tremble as she gathered her food wrapper for the garbage.

Mary rose along with her. "You stuck up for me," she said quickly. "Sort of. That day."

Bethany had her back to her and she stopped and stood near the garbage. "I didn't do a very good job."

"You did something."

She turned. "No, not really. I just…I hate it here, and some days I don't know whether to swim in the back of the pack of piranhas or go off on my own and hope they don't turn on me."

"Why would they turn on you?"

Bethany held her gaze for a long moment but gave away nothing. "They just would."

Mary felt her anxiety, could sense it resonating from her body. Feeling it from another was unusual, and it fell on her as if it was her own, weighing her down with sadness and helplessness. She couldn't stand there and watch someone else feel like shit for ridiculous reasons just like she had for years.

"Come here." She tugged gently on her hand and when they were face-to-face, Mary embraced her for a long, soft hug. "Whatever it is, it's okay. You just have to say fuck them and do your thing."

"I don't think I can. I don't think I can do that like you can."

"Yes, you can."

"You're brave."

Mary pulled away and laughed. "I am so not brave."

Bethany wiped a stray tear from her eye. "Yes, you are."

"No. I just got fed up with being afraid. Fuck these people, you know? I'm not going to continue to give them the power to ruin my day. If they want to make fun of me, that's fine. I hold my head high and breeze past them. If I hear them, I confront them. It's funny how many of them back down when I do that. A little spine goes a long way with jerks like that." Mary smiled softly at her. "Okay?"

"Yes."

"And if you ever need to talk—"

But Bethany interrupted her by leaning in and pressing her lips to Mary's. Mary stood still in shock and surprise. Once she realized what was happening, she backed away and searched Bethany's face for answers.

"You're—"

"Yes." She looked frantic suddenly. "I thought you were too."

"I—yes. I am." They stared at each other for a few long seconds, and before Mary could say anything else, the door opened and Wade waltzed in. He stopped and smiled, surprised at seeing them.

"Mary, Mary—"

"Fuck off, Wade," she said quickly, her feelings of empathy and understanding for Bethany gone in an instant, replaced by anger and contempt for Wade and the others.

"Whoa. What gives?"

Bethany moved away. "I need to go."

"Bethany, don't." She wanted to finish talking to her. She had dozens of questions, both for Bethany and herself.

"Did I interrupt something?" Wade asked with a smirk, not even trying to act polite.

Mary gave him a hard look. "You interrupted our conversation."

"Apparently." He laughed as he walked to the snack machine. "If you want privacy to make out or whatever, you need to go in the janitor's closet. Everybody knows that."

Bethany's face showed her fear and Wade just stood there popping peanut M&Ms in his mouth.

"Thanks for the tip," Mary said. "I'm surprised you know about the closet considering no one in this office has ever gone in there with you."

He studied her quietly for a moment like a great fighter considering if someone new was a worthy opponent or not.

"You're incorrect, Mary. I don't know who your sources are—"

"If you're talking about Carla, save it."

He lowered his snack and his eyes took on a serious look.

"We've all heard about that and it doesn't count."

"Well, what you heard—"

"I really don't want to repeat what I heard. Because it would only embarrass you and it would make me a gossip. So I won't go there."

"What did you hear?"

Mary turned to Bethany and opened the door. She held it for her and followed her out, leaving Wade alone and speechless in the break room.

"What did you hear?" Bethany asked as she exhaled long and slow.

"Nothing good. Just more office bullshit. Something about him not being able to get it up."

They headed toward Mary's desk and a few of their colleagues gave them curious glances.

"Thanks for that," Bethany said. "I think he's probably still standing there wondering what happened."

"I'm sure I'll pay for it later." They rounded her cubicle and Mary sank into her chair. "That's the thing about changing and standing up for yourself. At first, they're shocked and a little quiet. After the shock wears off, they come full force. Some quiet and sneaky, others loud and in your face."

"Then how do you stand to keep doing it?"

"I don't have a choice. This is who I am. I won't go back to hiding from everyone. I can't."

Bethany seemed uncomfortable and twirled her hair with a nervous hand. "I don't want to hide either, but I'm also very private."

"So don't say anything. No one needs to know your business. But don't let them walk all over you either." She caught sight of her voice message light. It was blinking. "I gotta get back to work."

"Oh, okay."

"I'll see you later."

She still looked uncomfortable and she looked around carefully before she left as if making sure no one was watching her. As soon as she left the cubicle, Mary slipped on her headset and listened to her voice mail. Disappointment spread through her like a dark disease. Jude hadn't called.

She tore off her headset and sat with her head in her hands. She was angry at herself for still getting so upset. She sighed and leaned back in her chair. Wade stormed by, bumping into someone. He cussed at them and continued on, looking to be headed toward Carla's office. Mary thought back to what he almost walked in on. Bethany had kissed her.

It was almost surreal, but it had happened.

She'd been so surprised by it she'd failed to really feel anything. She remembered the sudden press of Bethany's lips, the scent of her spicy perfume, and then the terrified look on her face when they'd pulled apart. Mary did remember feeling a jolt of excitement for a second as the realization had set in.

It didn't even come close to how it felt with Jude. But maybe the lack of instant lust she'd felt with Bethany was because she hadn't been able to give her a real chance.

Mary thought she was attractive and she seemed sincere. Why hadn't she noticed her before? She knew the answer. It was because she'd been one of them. Or at least seemed to be one of them. Was she?

Mary panicked, wondering if the whole thing could've been a setup? Her insides hardened. Was Bethany off telling the others right now?

Oh, God.

Stop it. Just stop.

She logged back into her computer, needing to return to work. Her paranoia obviously wasn't taking a backseat to her new attitude. She slipped her headset on again and was just about to dial into her phone to accept a new call when Bethany reappeared.

"Uh, hi." She still looked nervous, but her voice had a secret excitement to it. A small folded square of paper fell from her hand and onto Mary's desk. "See you later." And she rushed away, leaving only the scent of perfume behind.

Curious and more than a little relieved at seeing her there rather than off gossiping, Mary opened the paper. The message was written in pencil.

Meet me in the janitor's closet.

Mary stared at it, convinced she'd read it wrong. Then she stood and looked around. Everyone was hard at work, taking calls. Those that weren't were walking with purpose, unconcerned with her.

She stared at the block writing. There were no names, no other clues on the paper.

It was a joke. A setup.

Was it?

Her legs began to move, ignoring her paranoia. She crossed the room, wadding up the note as she went. It was a joke. It had to be. No one just up and kissed someone at work and then slipped them a note telling them to meet in the closet for a make out session. This wasn't junior high.

She walked quicker, determined to give whoever was behind it a piece of her mind. She was so sick of this. Just so, so sick of it.

The closet was off near a corner, on the same wall the restrooms were in. She opened it with strong force, not bothering to make sure no one was looking. Bethany was inside, standing in the dim light. Mary closed the door and confronted her.

"What the hell is this? I don't need this shit, Bethany. Who put you up to this? Wade? Meeker? Or did you come up with this one on your own?"

Mary couldn't see her face very well, just her outline. "What?"

"You think I'm stupid enough to fall for all that crap you dished in the break room?"

"Crap?"

"You're all in on this aren't you? Thought getting me to admit I'm gay would be funny?"

"No. Mary, I—there's—this is just me."

The light seeping under the door began to rest on Bethany's face.

"I wanted to be alone with you."

Mary swallowed as her pulse sped up. "You did?"

"Yes."

"Why?"

"Because I'm attracted to you."

Mary had never considered such a thing, especially at work. She wasn't sure what to say, even though the kiss in the break room had been a big clue. Her fucking paranoia had made her misread a situation and led her down the wrong path. Again.

"I always have been. I've just been too big of a coward to do anything about it." She touched Mary's face, and her palm was so warm and soft it threatened to melt Mary. Then she leaned in and kissed her again, this time with more passion, with lips that were as hot as her hand and more agile than her long fingers.

Mary found herself getting caught up in it, the kiss, the woman, the fact that she wanted her. It was nice. And forbidden. She kissed her back and they deepened their embrace and sought with awakening tongues. In an instant, Mary was alive and burning and pushing the limits of control.

She turned Bethany and pinned her to the door, and Bethany fumbled to lock it. Mary reattached to her lips, drawing in the lower one as she unbuttoned her pants and sank her hand inside.

"What are you—"

"Shh. Let me touch you." Mary had to make her come. She had to hear her fall to pieces in her ear.

A hiss came from her as Mary stroked her slick knot of flesh.

"Oh God," she whispered. "Mary."

"Does it feel good?" She nibbled on her neck as she pressed into her over and over.

"Yes."

She tried for Mary's slacks, but Mary wasn't ready for that.

"No. Just you."

"Why?"

"I—" Mary had no answer. She just knew she couldn't allow Bethany to touch her like that. Was this what Jude felt like? The thought clouded her mind and toyed with her, reminding her that this wasn't Jude. Bethany didn't feel like Jude or smell like her or sound like her.

Groaning, Mary increased the speed of her hand and buried her face in Bethany's hair. Bethany muted her own sounds by kissing and sucking on Mary's neck.

"Mary," she said. "Oh, Mary."

Short, throaty "ahs" pushed into Mary's ear as Bethany moved beneath her hand. She came quickly and clung to Mary tightly.

With her eyes closed, Mary gave to her until she went limp and stilled. After a few silent moments, she laughed softly and kissed her way up Mary's neck to her face. "That was intense. I don't think I've ever come that fast."

She tried to kiss her lips, but Mary turned her face and backed away.

"What is it?" Bethany's tone had changed. She was worried and Mary sensed it and felt horrible, knowing that this was what she felt when Jude pulled away from her.

"Nothing."

"Can I touch you?"

Suddenly, she could understand Jude's perspective and see her own in Bethany. Instead of comforting her, it left her feeling hollow inside. Jude felt like this? Jude didn't really want her? Didn't want her to touch her because of control and trust and lack of true desire? It all made sense.

She had been fooling herself in chasing after Jude.

"Mary?" Bethany was touching her face again. Her eyes were searching, looking desperately for the connection she'd thought they had. Mary couldn't stand to hurt her.

"I'm okay."

"You sure?"

"I will be." She silenced any further comment by kissing her. Bethany laughed in obvious delight and Mary welcomed her tongue with her own. The kiss grew deeper and hotter and Mary allowed her to unbutton and unzip her pants. She welcomed the gentle slide of Bethany's fingertips just like she had her tongue, by relaxing and just feeling.

Bethany knew exactly what she was doing, and soon Mary was leaning into her, supporting herself by placing her hands on the door.

"Yeah," Bethany said to her. "You feel spectacular."

Mary's eyes rolled back with pure pleasure, and again she buried her face in Bethany's hair.

"Spread your legs a little further for me," Bethany said. "Yes, like that. Ride my hand." And she plunged her fingers inside and stimulated her g-spot.

"Oh fuck," Mary said, closing her eyes.

"Feels good doesn't it?" She kissed her, swirling her tongue around hungrily. "I know it does."

And then her fingers came out, hot and coated with her slickness, and stroked her clit. Mary forced everything from her mind, insisting that the pleasure wash through her.

"Ah, oh God. Oh fuck." She rocked into her and Bethany sucked hard on her neck and Mary came, briefly losing control, bucking wildly, kissing Bethany forcefully, overtaking her with her tongue and groans. It took all her strength to remain upright, and when her hands squeaked as they started to slide down the door, it brought back memories of that first night with Jude when she had been the one up against the wall getting taken. It seized her—mind, soul, and body—and she leaned on Bethany as she shook with raw emotion and orgasmic aftershocks.

The release was bittersweet, just like Jude.

"Fuck." It seemed to be her favorite word lately. Somehow encompassing everything she was feeling when no other word possibly could.

Bethany held her and smoothed her back. She removed her hand from between Mary's legs slowly and sucked Mary off her fingers. "Spectacular," she whispered.

The sight stirred Mary, and even though a part of her wanted to kiss her wildly again, a bigger part of her wanted to leave, to escape the dark confines of the cold closet and drive home to snuggle safely in her bed where this mad, crazy, awakening world couldn't reach her and poke at her insides.

Bethany's eyes clouded with concern. "You're not okay are you?"

Mary fastened her pants.

"Please, just tell me."

"I—there's nothing to say. This was…fun."

"Then why do you look like you're scared shitless?"

Mary reached for the door. "I can't explain. Not right now."

"Can I see you? Outside of work?"

"I don't know." Tears threatened. "I don't think so."

"Why?"

Mary felt horrible. How could she do this to someone else when she knew how badly it hurt? "I'm confused, Bethany. And I think I'm in love with someone else."

"Then why do this?"

"I don't know. I'm such a mess." She held her hand. "Please don't take this wrong. You are amazing and beautiful. But I'm... lost."

"Can I call you then? Sometime?"

"You deserve someone far better, Bethany. Someone who has her head on straight and her heart free."

She turned the doorknob and slipped out, leaving Bethany standing there in the dim light.

CHAPTER FIFTEEN

Jude looked gaunt. At least according to Fran she did. Sickly. Like she hadn't seen the sun in weeks.

"Are you sick?" Fran crossed her long legs and sipped her coffee. Jude had refused one, not in the mood for much of anything.

"No."

"Depressed?"

Jude shuffled papers and pretended to stare at her computer.

Fran, as usual, honed in on her. "Ah ha. What is it? Life crisis, pet died, heartbreak?"

Jude shot her a look.

"I see."

"It's nothing."

"Whatever." She looked away and Jude could feel the change in her mood. A few seconds later, she stood.

"What's wrong?" Jude asked.

"What's wrong? Oh, nothing." She fastened her eyes to her. "Look, Jude, I know you're private and all that jazz. But I consider you a friend. One I can trust. I just wish you thought the same of me."

Jude exhaled and rubbed her forehead. "Sit. Please."

Fran hesitated but did. She didn't bother crossing her legs.

"I'm sorry."

"I don't want an apology, Jude. I want you to tell me what's going on. Did it ever occur to you that I might actually be able to help?"

Jude couldn't help but laugh.

"Is that funny?"

"No. Yes." She waved the comment off. "Fran, to tell you the truth I don't think you really would want to hear what is going on with me."

"Try me."

"You are sure?"

"Jesus, Jude. Come on."

With a long press of her lips, Jude leaned forward and steepled her fingers. "I don't know where to begin."

"Who is she? The one who has you all twisted up."

"Pardon?"

"Don't be coy. Tell me. Who is she? And if you say she's a student I will get up off this chair and slap you silly."

Jude stared at her in disbelief.

"I know you're gay, Jude. Get over yourself and tell me."

"You know?" She'd never said a word to anyone. Never hinted or joked or anything.

"Yes, I know. I also know that the sky is blue and that cactus out there is green. Come on, I'm not stupid."

"I didn't realize it was so obvious."

"No one talks about it if that's what you're worried about." She crossed her legs. "I know simply because of that."

"What?"

"You stare at my legs when I cross them."

Jude cleared her throat as if that would somehow help with the rush of sudden embarrassment. But she refused to look away from Fran's eyes.

"It's okay. It's natural. I work hard for these bad girls so I don't mind."

Nerves caused Jude to laugh a little. Women never made her nervous, but it seemed lots of things were changing in regard to women lately.

"She is a student," Jude said softly.

"Jude, no."

"Not one of mine and not young."

"Well, thank God."

"Her name is Mary."

"Mary. That sounds nice. Is she nice?"

Jude nodded. "Yes."

"Did you meet her here?"

Her chair squeaked a little as she leaned back, considering how to answer. "Not exactly." When she didn't say more, Fran moved on.

"So what's the problem? You like her, right?"

"Yes, I do. Very much. And that is the problem. I like her too much."

Fran laughed. "How is that a problem?"

"Because I like my life like it is."

"You mean your intensely private, predictable, and lonely life? That one?"

A smile came. One that held obvious amusement for Fran. "I am not lonely, Fran. That is, I never used to be. Nor is my life predictable. I have plenty of excitement."

"Then there's something you aren't telling me."

"Yes, there is."

"Okaay."

"I have many…liaisons."

Fran blinked. "Oh." She played with her straw, digging through her Frappuccino. "I wasn't expecting that one."

"Should I stop?"

"No." She was quick to answer. "At least one of us is getting some."

Jude laughed. "And I wasn't ready for that one."

They both laughed.

"Seriously, though, I'm glad you're telling me."

Jude fell silent for a long moment. It did feel good to bounce this off someone, even if it meant entrusting and giving up a little control.

"So why are you so messed up over this? You like her, but you obviously like your freedom. Just be honest with her and move on."

"I—I've tried. She's persistent and…" Jude rubbed her lips as she thought about the way Mary tasted. "I don't want it to stop."

Fran spoke softer, sensing Jude's truth. "So don't stop it then. Date her, be with her. Make it good. You deserve that, Jude."

"I don't think I can." Her voice cracked and she cleared her throat again and stood. The topic was causing some emotion to rise and she didn't like it.

"Jude? It's okay. Try to relax."

"I can't. This…this is doing something to me."

"It's making you feel."

She stared at her. "What?"

"I think you need to figure out what it is that's really stopping you from developing something with this woman. I don't think it's because you have numerous lovers. I think it's something more."

Jude crossed her arms and stared out the window.

"Do you know that in all the years I've known you, I've never seen you like this? Ever, Jude. So whoever she is, she's reached you. Touched you. And I think that's probably scaring the hell out of you."

"You cannot possibly know that." But it was true. Fran, in all her silent sleuth glory, had hit the nail right on the head.

"I'm not attacking you, Jude." Fran stood and came to her, setting her drink on the desk. "I'm your friend. I care." She touched her arm. "Whatever it is, you can tell me if you need to."

"I don't know," Jude whispered, her voice giving. It hurt, that horrible burning rushing up through her.

"Come here." Fran turned her and enveloped her in a tight hug.

Jude didn't return the hug at first, but when Fran began to stroke her hair and tell her that it was okay, she not only returned the hug, she felt like she might cry. She clung tighter to Fran, trying to force the tears back down.

"I hate feeling like this," she said. "I hate crying."

"Sometimes you need to."

"No."

"Jude, let it out."

"I cannot." But the pain was unbearable. It was burning and cinching up her throat. Her lungs felt full of acid. "It hurts." She'd never cried in front of another, rarely cried even on her own. She didn't want to start with Fran.

"Let it out. It needs to come out. You shouldn't hold pain inside. It eats away at you."

Jude stepped away. She couldn't cry in front of her. The shame and lack of strength would haunt her for weeks. "I have to go." She grabbed her tote and fumbled for her keys. Fran seemed to understand.

"Go home and let it out. You'll feel better."

Jude had to force out acid-coated words. "I will try."

"If you need me, you know where to find me."

Jude swallowed painfully and nodded. "Thank you."

She left and headed for her car. Boxing, hiking, lifting the free weights at home, none of it would help. She considered going to Conquest. She hadn't been in a week. Would conquering woman after woman help? She could do it. Fuck someone's brains out. But it wouldn't be the same. She wouldn't care; she wouldn't feel anything like she normally did. Her own excitement wouldn't build, wouldn't burn, wouldn't explode.

Only Mary could make her feel the passion she craved. But she didn't know if she could let someone in. Tears began to build again, and she drove slowly, wondering if Mary was thinking of her. She'd seen her around campus, wearing nicer clothes, walking with a confident, strong gait. She didn't seem to be missing Jude and she hadn't come looking for her at the college either. Was it all a part of her new game? Should she call her? Mary would win for sure if she did, and Jude couldn't handle just being a part of another game. It had crushed her before, scarred her for life. She couldn't be someone's toy when she had real feelings for her.

A red light hovered ahead. To head home she needed to get in the right lane. But home wasn't where she wanted to go. She couldn't stand another night of grading papers and staring at her parakeet. She dug in her tote for her phone and called Conquest.

It was after five and hopefully Cord would already be there. He answered on the third ring.

"Yeah?"

"Cord."

"Yeah."

"Has anyone been asking for me?"

She could hear him breathing and she imagined him hauling ice and beer, readying the bar for the night.

"Lately?"

"Within the last week. Has anyone called or come by asking for me?"

"Like that woman? What's her name, Mary?"

She hesitated as more control fled like an unraveling ribbon in the wind. "Yes."

He didn't say anything for a few seconds, probably as shocked as she was at the admission.

"No. Not since last time."

No? Nothing? Mary really was serious. She wanted Jude to come to her. "Okay."

"You gonna come back?"

She turned left and headed away from home. "I don't know."

"If she calls, I'll let you know."

She hung up, unable to respond. There was no point in going to Conquest. Mary wouldn't be there. There was only one other option, and since Mary didn't have class, Jude had a pretty good chance of catching her.

She pulled into a gas station and searched for Mary's address on her cell phone. It came up right away, and to her relief, it wasn't far from where she was.

The air in the car grew stifling as she sat and contemplated her next move.

Going to Mary's was risky, desperate, and it guaranteed nothing. It would only make her look like the seeking lonely fool, and she'd sworn to herself she'd never go back to that. But what else was she going to do? She was a wreck. A hollow, pale wreck, and people had noticed. Everyone but Mary. She seemed to be doing just fine.

Jude rubbed her temples. What if Mary had moved on? The possibility was like a hard slap to her face. Worse than the punch she'd taken from the boxer, which still had her jaw sore.

She trembled as more tears built up inside. Something had to be done. She put the car in drive and sped to Mary's neighborhood. It didn't take her long to find her house. It was newer but small with a mauve Spanish tile roof and white stucco walls. A Chevy Aveo was parked in the drive.

Jude grew more nervous as she parked along the side of the street. The nerves drove her crazy, just like the uncontrollable longing and verging tears. She took a deep breath and walked with her head high to the front door. The doorbell was loud and she shoved her hands into her slacks and steeled herself for composure.

Several moments passed and she could've taken off. Mary would've never known it was her, but she wasn't a quitter or a hider. She was strong, even if she didn't feel that way.

The door opened a crack, slowly.

"Jude?" It opened further and showed a well dressed Mary in a lavender mock turtleneck and stylish gray slacks. She still had on makeup and Jude found herself focused on her beautiful rich lips. She was stunning.

"Hello."

Mary appeared shocked and she seemed to be at a loss for words. "What—I'm surprised to see you here."

"Forgive me, but I looked up your address."

"No, it's fine, it's fine. Would you like to come in?" She pulled the door open further.

"I will get right to the point. I…I want to see you."

Mary again seemed overcome with surprise.

"You did say I had to come to you, didn't you?"

"Yes. Yes, I did."

"Would you like to see me?"

"I—Jude please come in." She wrapped her hand around Jude's and tugged. Jude inhaled at how hot and soft it was. Mary noticed, and after she closed the door she released her. "Are you okay?"

Laughter tumbled out of Jude, but it sounded awkward and forced. Her body continued to shake even after she stopped.

"Jude?" Mary touched her again.

Oh fuck, her resolve was crumbling.

"Don't," she said walking away from her. "I cannot have you touching me."

"Why?"

Jude stood behind the sofa. "Look, I just want to see you."

Mary hugged herself as if she were cold. "Okay."

"I came over here to say that. That is all." It wasn't all, but she didn't yet have the strength to express the rest.

"Would you like to sit down? Have a drink maybe?"

"A drink, yes." She had to calm down. Hearing that Mary wanted to see her was great, but there was so much more racking her insides. And the way Mary was looking at her...Jesus. She had been a fool to think she could handle this. "Wait. No. I had better go."

Mary crossed to her quickly as she moved back toward the door.

"You don't have to go."

"I do."

"Please don't." Mary stepped in front of her and pressed her hands to her shoulders. "Jude," she said softly. "Please don't go. Not yet. You just got here and..." She touched her face and her impossibly hot hands felt like they were penetrating her bones. Mary brushed her thumb over her lip. "What happened? Did you hurt yourself?"

"Yes." She had hurt herself. She'd stepped in the ring and fought someone she was nowhere near qualified to fight.

"How?"

"It doesn't matter."

"You got in a fight? At Conquest?" Worry wrinkled her face.

"No. It was stupid. I was trying—"

She breathed deeply again.

"Trying to what?"

"I was trying to forget about you."

"Oh." Mary's eyes sparkled as if they had filled with tiny diamonds.

"It was stupid. It didn't work." Jude trembled as she blew out a long breath. "Nothing has worked. And I shouldn't be telling you this."

"Why not?" Mary's voice was low and her eyelids heavy with obvious desire. She rubbed her body against Jude's.

"Because."

"Because you don't like admitting such feelings?" She was a breath away and Jude could smell everything about her, from her perfume to her shampoo to the sweetness of her mouth.

"Yes."

Mary kissed her. Very lightly. Touching her lips softly with delicate, warm presses. "You're trembling. Do I make you nervous?"

Jude didn't answer, but instead kissed her back. She tasted as sweet as the scent of her had promised and Jude went deeper, slipping her tongue inside to dance with Mary's.

"Ah," Mary said between the long kisses. "I've missed you."

Jude walked her to the couch where she lifted Mary and placed her along the back. "You have?"

"Oh God, yes."

It was heavenly music to her ears and her body heated instantaneously. She held her and kissed her harder, loving the feel of her slick tongue. "How much?"

Mary laughed. "You really want to know?"

"Yes."

"Here." Mary took her hand and shoved it down her slacks. Jude felt the heat of her flesh through her panties. "Go inside," Mary said, helping her slip inside her underwear. "There," she purred. "You feel that? That's how much I missed you."

Jude groaned. Mary was as hot and slick as her tongue was and she grew even more so as Jude stroked her. "Fuck, Mary."

"Yes," Mary said.

Jude allowed the desire to overcome her. Mary was ready and waiting, begging for her to continue. It was better than her dreams. And suddenly she couldn't believe she'd gone this long without inhaling her, touching her, tasting her.

"My mouth must be on you. On all of you. Now." She tugged up on Mary's sweater and with her help, she lifted it over her head. They kissed again with hungry tongues and Mary gasped as Jude squeezed her clitoris and went to kiss her neck.

Jude loved the smell of her skin and her moist hair at the base of her neck. She was about to close her eyes and feast when she saw a dark red mark. Her blood froze and she pulled away. The mark was unmistakable. It had been made by a mouth. A hungry mouth. Someone else's mouth.

"No," she let out, stumbling backward. Mary cried out in surprise as Jude's hand left her flesh. Jude fumbled against the two barstools behind her, crashing onto her backside.

"What? Oh my God, what?" Mary hopped off the back of the couch and hurried toward her. "Jude? What is it? What's wrong?"

Jude scrambled to her feet and pushed her hands away. She clenched her eyes as the shock gave way and the unbearable pain set in. It hurt like nothing had before, and she thought she might fall to the floor and pass out.

"Jude!" Mary sounded frantic and Jude continued to push her away. She opened her eyes, but she couldn't look at her.

She couldn't withstand her beauty and scent and see the mark destroying it all.

Jude hurried toward the door as Mary realized why she was so upset. "Oh my God. Oh my God," she said softly and rushed toward her, trying to wedge herself between Jude and the door. "Jude. Jude, please listen. It was nothing. Nothing! It was just— oh God, fuck—I don't know, a woman at work. She came on to me and we—it didn't last long and it was just one time."

Jude could barely speak and she kept her eyes trained on the door.

"That mark is more than a kiss." Jude winced as she imagined another inhaling Mary's skin, sucking on it, tasting it.

"It was a one-time thing. I don't have any feelings for her. Jude, please."

"I cannot bear to look at you," she whispered.

Mary held her face and gently turned it. "Jude, look at me. Look into my eyes. I want *you*."

But another scenario was more likely. Mary had gotten a taste for sex, for women, and she was experimenting, trying out new things and other women. It explained her new attitude and confidence. It made sense, and Jude could hardly blame her.

But she couldn't be a part of that. Her swelling heart and uncontrollable feelings wouldn't allow it.

"I have to go," Jude said.

"No." Mary's expression went from one of fear and concern to one of confusion. "Why do I get in trouble for making out with someone for two minutes while you're fucking a different woman every night?"

"You are mistaken."

"Am I?"

"Yes."

"Two a night?"

"It isn't like that." Not anymore.

"Because it doesn't exactly make sense."

"I don't expect you to understand." Who would? Jude's life may have been simple with a bit of a well controlled wild side, but to others it must seem completely risqué and irresponsible. And now, with the way it was all changing inside her, she really couldn't expect Mary to understand.

"Good, because I don't."

All she'd done was try to prevent this madness.

"Let me go. Let me go before—" But the rising emotion finally overtook her and she collapsed against the door and sobbed. The pain was horrible and all-consuming and she hated that she was doing it in front of Mary and it just made the tears come all the heavier.

Mary tried to turn her, to soothe her, but Jude refused to move from the door, keeping her forehead firmly pressed to it. She didn't like the noises she was making or the pinched look her face must have had. She couldn't control her breathing or the trembling of her body. Yet she didn't have the strength to pull the door open and flee.

"Jude, Jude, come here." Mary was trying to turn her again, but Jude refused, pounding the door with her fist.

"I'm sorry, Jude. I didn't know you wanted me. I didn't know anything. I thought you just wanted sex."

"Just—" Jude tried. "Just leave me alone."

"I don't want to. You're crying, for God's sake. Just let me hold you."

"No. I cannot. Please, just for a few moments. I need to be alone."

She felt Mary's hand fall from her back and heard her walk away. Jude tried to take big breaths and calm down, but she wasn't quite ready yet. Her body had more emotion to purge. The tears felt like fiery bindings squeezing her lungs, and it hurt like hell to let them out. But she knew she couldn't keep them in any longer. They had been hatched and there was no way to keep them contained.

She pounded the door again as the feelings rushed out. Fear. Loss of control. Vulnerability. Betrayal. And then more came. All the things she feared exposing herself to. Tenderness. Meaning. Love. Trust. Touching.

"Jude?" Mary was back and calling to her softly. "You don't have to say anything. I just want you to know that it's always been you that I wanted."

Jude wiped her eyes and turned. She drew a deep breath and leaned against the door for support. Mary looked frightened and worried and compassionate.

"The only reason why I dressed up like I did and seduced you like that was so that you would want to see me. Even though I wanted you and I wanted so much more than sex, I was willing to give up the rest just so you would continue touching me. And I had hoped that someday you would let me touch you too."

Jude still couldn't speak, but Mary's words, just like the mere sight of her, touched her deep inside. Mary had put her mock turtleneck back on and she was standing there wringing her hands, worrying herself crazy over a woman she hardly knew, but she obviously cared very much about.

Most people would give anything for such a woman. But Jude had fought it and run from her, while still taking Mary's body to satisfy her own selfish need to feel her and consume her.

"I'm sorry," Jude finally said and her lungs ceased burning and the fog in her mind cleared.

"Don't be. Everyone cries."

"I'm sorry for crying, yes. But mostly I'm sorry for the way I have treated you."

"You were honest with me. That's more than most. And you never asked to get involved, that was all me." She came closer. "I'm not worried about that though. I'm more curious about why this upset you so much." She lightly touched her neck where the mark was hidden beneath her shirt.

"Is it not obvious?"

"Is it because you—"

"Because I am selfish." This time Jude took a step toward Mary. "It is just me being selfish, just like I always am."

"How so?"

Jude whispered, the words so powerful that if she said them any louder they would've knocked her over. "I want you, Mary. For myself. I don't like to think about you with another. I cannot *bear* to think about it."

"You can't?"

"No."

"But you still want freedom for yourself?"

"No." Jude rushed toward her. "Mary, I only want you. I have tried with others and no one—there is only you." She touched Mary's face. "Knowing this, accepting this. It has nearly killed me."

Mary stared deeply into her eyes and swallowed. "Me too."

Jude smiled, so moved by her. She trembled. "And I'm so afraid."

"I know," Mary said softly, holding Jude's hands to her face. "I know."

"I haven't—there hasn't been anyone in a long time. Years."

"Someone hurt you."

Jude shook her head. "It is stupid. Old wounds."

"I won't hurt you."

Jude kissed her softly. "You cannot possibly promise that, Mary."

"I can."

"No, but it doesn't matter."

Mary kissed her fingertips. "What does matter?"

"This. Right here, right now." She kissed her and they melded together, capturing and holding and tasting. "And you. Only you." Jude held her closer, tighter, running her hands up and down her back, searching for bare skin. When she found it she groaned and lifted the shirt off her once again.

"You're better than any fantasy I have ever had," Jude said as she gently kissed her shoulders, thumbing away the straps of her bra. "I have been a fool to deny it."

Mary sighed with awakening pleasure. "Jude," she said and then clung to her with her arms and eager mouth.

Jude lifted her and hurried down the hall, stopping against the wall a few times along the way to gain her balance and devour Mary further.

"In here," Mary said breathlessly, pointing.

Jude carried her to the bed and set her down. Then she latched on to her neck and bit softly. "Mary."

Mary's nails dug into her skin and Jude arched into her, trying to ease her onto her back. But Mary resisted, wanting instead to undress Jude. She did so by starting at the base of her blouse, unbuttoning it slowly all the way up. Her mouth followed her hands as they slid along opening the edges, revealing a toned path of tingling skin. Jude sighed as Mary's lips welcomed her, kissing her torso as they traveled all the way up. When they reached Jude's mouth, they teased, a long pink tongue darting out at her lips.

Mary laughed just like she had the night Jude had seduced her, and it sent a bolt of desire right up her spine. Mary felt her react and she halted after tugging on Jude's lower lip. "Is this okay?" she asked. "Me being aggressive?"

Jude made a noise of approval and squeezed her tightly. "God, yes. You never have to ask."

Mary grinned. "So my sexy persona didn't scare you away any?"

"Nein." She hugged her tighter and Mary laughed. "You are sexy all the time."

"In that case…" Mary pushed away and walked to the side of the bed where she turned back the covers and lit the two candles on her nightstand. Then as Jude watched, she stripped completely and curled her finger at her, beckoning.

Jude walked up to her, her mouth already watering at the way the candlelight was dancing on Mary's skin. She bent to kiss her again, but Mary stopped her with a gentle finger. "Wait."

Mary's eyes were large and soulful and they took Jude in and held her. Safely, warmly. Her hands dropped to undress Jude, starting with her bra and finishing with her slacks and shoes. She motioned at the bed. "Lie down."

A few nerves fluttered and Jude hesitated.

"Please. Before I make you."

Jude laughed softly. "Okay." The sheets felt cool against her back, but she warmed up quickly as Mary slid in next to her and wrapped her in her arms.

"I bet you're wondering what it is I plan on doing to you."

"You would be correct."

"Mm. Should I tell you? How about I just show you?" Jude watched Mary's hand as it trailed up and down the center of her abdomen, just like her mouth had when she'd unbuttoned her shirt.

Jude's body responded at once and she lifted up into her, unable to remain still.

"Feel good?" Mary asked, whispering in her ear.

"Yes."

"Good. Because that's what this is all about. I want to make you feel as good as I do when you touch me."

Jude licked her lips as her heart raced. She wanted it. She so badly wanted it. But could she really relax and take it?

"It will be okay," Mary said, kissing her ear, her jaw, her lips. "Here." She took Jude's hands and placed them on her bare breasts so Jude was holding herself. Then she propped herself up on one arm and placed her hand on Jude's. Lightly, delicately, she touched Jude's skin through the gaps of her fingers.

"If at any time you want me to stop, you need to say so. No other word will do."

Jude laughed. "I won't need to."

"Ah, my darling Jude, you cannot possibly know such a thing."

Jude reached up and stroked her hair. It was dancing and shimmering. She was so beautiful and so full of life. "I want you, Mary. All of you. That means knowing you."

Mary kissed her hand. "Quit it. Any more talk like that and I'll lose my patience and eat you alive."

"In that case…"

"Oh no, you don't." Mary straddled her and shrieked when Jude tried to tickle her. "Quit it!" But she was laughing so hard she could hardly protest.

After battling for a few seconds, she was finally able to pin Jude's hands above her head. "There." She was breathless and flushed and Jude was so turned on she could feel herself throbbing. "Now where was I?"

"You were just about to eat me alive."

"Oh no. Not so fast." She released her hands and brought them back down to where they were before. "I touch you only where you touch you."

Jude tried to speak.

"No, don't argue." She repeated the touch from before, touching her skin between the gaps of her fingers. "Like that. And if you want more, or a different spot, just move your hand."

Jude immediately moved her hands and framed her nipples, causing Mary to laugh.

"You move fast, Professor Jaeger." She skimmed her fingers across her taut nipples and Jude hissed with pleasure.

"I like it when you call me that," she said.

"I like it too."

She bent and licked Jude's fingers, beginning with the tops and then lowering to rim the insides. Jude had done the same to her when she'd touched herself at Conquest. The sensation was breathtaking. And when she reached her nipples, Jude came up off the bed and kissed her madly. Mary cried out and pinched her nipples. Jude clawed at her back, pushing her tongue into her again and again.

Mary tore herself away and panted.

But Jude didn't wait for her to speak. "Touch me," she said. "Now."

She leaned back and took hold of Mary's hands. She led them all over her upper body and down to where Mary was straddling her.

"Are you sure?"

This was the moment Jude had been thinking about for weeks. And now that it was here, there was no denying the way she felt. It was what her body wanted, what her mind wanted, what her heart wanted. She looked into Mary's eyes and nodded. "I feel like I'm going to die if you don't."

Mary stared so passionately at her Jude thought she might burst into flames. And then she whispered, "Baby," and lowered herself, pressing Jude open with firm palms to her inner thighs.

She breathed on her heavily and then attached her mouth and tongued her through her panties.

Jude shouted and lifted herself, tangling her hands in Mary's hair. "Oh, fuck, Mary," she said watching her and going insane. "Fuck, it feels so good."

Mary tugged harder and then flattened her tongue and licked her, sneaking her tongue into the sides to tease her bare flesh. Jude called out and held her tighter, then lay back to push herself up into her.

"Hurry, Mary. Hurry. I'm afraid I might hurt you." Her fingers were already painfully tight and her body was so alive and rigid with want there was no telling what her strength might bring.

Mary stopped and hurriedly helped tear her panties off. She looked hungry and driven, thirsty for Jude's flesh. She held her gaze for a long moment before dipping her head and taking in all of her.

"Ahhhh fuuuck meee." Jude's eyes rolled and closed. The pleasure was so great it was almost unbearable, and she thought for sure she would die right there with Mary sucking her off. "Fuuuck." It was all she could say, and when Mary stroked her with her slick tongue while she held her tightly in her mouth, Jude almost cried in sheer ecstasy. Words were gone and her brain was molten pleasure. All she could do was pump herself into her and squeeze her hands in Mary's hair. And it got better and better and Mary moaned into her and Jude went insane with need.

"Hurry. Oh, please."

But Mary released her and looked up at her with dancing eyes. Then she focused on Jude's flesh and snaked out her tongue to rim her clitoris. She circled it over and over and Jude whimpered, helpless.

"Mary," she cried.

"Yes."

"Please."

"Like this?" She licked at her slowly. Full tongue pressing over her for a miniscule second.

"Mm."

She quickened her rhythm and pressed harder.

"Yes!"

Then she stopped and took her clit in her mouth with wet, puckered lips. She sucked hard and then released her to lick. She continued the pattern until Jude couldn't control herself anymore.

"Mary, please, now!"

"Please what, baby? Tell me."

"More," she said. "Oh God, more. Mary, please, more. And don't stop. Ah, fuck, don't stop."

Mary reattached to her with a pleasurable moan, taking her in to suck and lick at the same time.

Jude tugged on her hair, ensuring she couldn't back away, and she pumped harder, faster, and clung to Mary like she was clinging to life. And then her climax crushed her back into the bed, tightening all her muscles for several blissfully long seconds, tearing through her body like an erotic virus set loose within her blood. She loved it, oh dear God, how she loved it, and when it finally blew away like a quick breath of air to a candle, she opened her eyes and focused on Mary who was lying between her legs with the most beautiful look she'd ever seen on a woman.

"Hi," she said and grinned.

Jude waved, her voice tight. "Hi."

"I suddenly feel shy."

Jude laughed. "Shy? Come here."

Mary crawled up and laid next to her and Jude covered them both with the sheet and then snuggled into her, wrapping her in her arms.

"What are you thinking?"

"That was…" Mary started. "Jude, if anybody could experience what I just experienced, they'd be lined up out the door at Conquest twenty-four seven."

Jude chuckled and bit her shoulder playfully. "That's how it is for me when I see you climax. I don't know how you got this far in life without a slew of lovers."

"I don't want a slew of lovers. I don't think I ever would've wanted that."

Jude brushed a hair from her cheek.

"And I don't want them lined out the door at Conquest."

"You don't?"

"No." She kissed her lips. "There isn't going to be any more Conquest."

Mary held her face and searched her eyes.

"All I want and need is right here."

"You're sure?"

"Yes."

Mary beamed at her and her eyes filled with tears. "Jude, I don't want to scare you, but—"

"But what?"

"Nothing." She wiped her eyes and shook her head. "Nothing. I'm just glad you're here. I'm just so glad you're here." She kissed her and when it deepened, she moaned and straddled Jude once again.

"Oh no," Jude said playfully as she sat up.

"Oh yes." Mary wrapped herself around her and tugged on her lips with hungry teeth and tongue. "Fuck me. With your fingers, right now." She pulled away a little and Jude slid her hand down her front to her center. It was slick and waiting and when she went inside, Mary threw her head back and groaned.

"Oh, Jude. Oh, beautiful Jude."

She came back up and looked in her eyes as she began to move her hips. "Fuck me, baby. Fuck me all night long."

Jude kissed her and tightened her grip on her lower back as she curled her fingers against her. She was tight and wet around her. She was beautiful and flushed and moving against her.

No, there was no other place on earth Jude would've rather been.

"I will, Mary," she said, putting her mouth to her neck. "I will."

CHAPTER SIXTEEN

It was already dark when Mary pulled up to Conquest. The one streetlight hummed and struggled just like it had the first night she'd come to the club. That night seemed like a million years ago and so too did the anxiety she'd felt.

Crossing the parking lot, her high heels clicked and her tight leather skirt swished a little against her backside. A man near the door grinned and nodded to her as he lit up and she waved to him even though he was bare-assed and still a little creepy.

Nothing in the club scared her now, and when she stepped in the door and saw and heard the roar of laughter from her colleagues, she didn't run off or burn with embarrassment and shame. Instead, anger and amusement passed through her.

"What the fuck are you doing here?" she asked, making her way to the bar. Though slightly unnerved, she hid it well and downed a shot of tequila.

"Us? What about you?"

"Holy shit! She's really here!"

"In fishnets and stilettos!"

There appeared to be five or six of them, most of them men. Mary remained calm and ordered another shot of tequila from Cord who was giving her a curious look. She knew he was about to blow, and from the looks of the guys sitting at the bar, he wasn't the only one.

Mary slung back her shot and turned to face them. As she did she saw Bethany and Carla Meeker in the far corner. Both were watching her. She crossed to them slowly, surprised at seeing Bethany.

"Ladies," she said. "Enjoying yourselves?" They were holding hands and Mary wasn't sure if it was out of fear or something more.

Bethany was quick to speak. "I had no idea where we were going. They just said we were going out for a drink."

"Well, why don't we have one? On me?"

Carla just stared at her, eyes wide. She kept looking Mary up and down, and Mary was amused. She'd never seen Carla so quiet before.

"Or maybe not." She turned back to the men. They were taking bets and talking about who Mary would get it on with. She was surprised at how calm she still was. At how meaningless these men and what they thought were. Still…she did have to work with them.

"You assholes need to go," Cord suddenly belted, silencing them.

Mary approached. "Wait a minute. They had the card, right?"

He gave her a hard look and eventually nodded. A man at the bar spoke. "One of 'em did."

"Which one?" Mary asked.

Wade's face fell as they all pointed to him. Mary walked up and held out her hand. "Let's see it, Wade."

He glared at her and refused. But Cord rounded the bar and dug it out for him, fished it right out of his back pocket. It appeared to be well used and it had a name scrawled on the back.

"Night."

Mary called out over the music, and there Night appeared in all his unisex glory. His sidekick Sky, who wore a mask, slinked up to Mary and hung off her side. The sight of them brought back visions from her first night, and that same excitement rushed through her again.

"The fresh one," he hissed at her, trying to lean in and kiss her. She pushed him away, excited but not interested.

"It's not my card," she said. "It's his." She pointed to Wade. Night quickly sized him up.

"Oh, him."

Mumbles and some laughter came from her colleagues.

"He's been here before?" she asked, trying to hide her surprise.

"Yes."

"He's been with you?"

Night looked at Cord who crossed his beefy arms and nodded. Night answered. "Yes. He only likes me. Says he likes little men."

There were gasps all around. Mary fed the card back to Wade who stood looking completely shocked and embarrassed. She moved to the rest of the guys.

"Was this enough of a show for you?" None of them held her gaze and every single one of them looked uncomfortable. She nodded a thanks to Cord who ordered them out. She couldn't help but smile a little in victory. She'd faced up to them and showed no fear while being exactly who she was. She was proud of herself.

"Hey, Mary," Cord called to her as she headed down the hallway. She turned. "Those two chicks that were with them, they wanna stay."

"Really?"

"Yeah. They wanna go off to a room together with Sky."

"Wow."

"Are they gonna give me trouble?"

Meeker and Bethany. She shrugged. "I don't think so. Watch the blonde one though."

"The tart with the fake tits?"

"Yes. She's a bit—"

"Hyper?"

She nodded. He threw up his hands and walked away mumbling to himself.

Mary faced Jude's door. With a deep breath, she entered without knocking and Jude jumped out of her skin.

"Mary, Jesus." She was holding a leather vest and had it gripped to her chest.

"Sorry, I know the red sign is up," she said, grinning.

"That's okay," Jude said with a low, seriously interested voice. Her eyes traveled over her several times. "What are you wearing?"

"Oh, just a little something I felt like trying on." She edged the room slowly, letting Jude take her in. "What are you up to?" The room had been cleared of personal items, leaving only the bed and dresser.

Jude finally tore her eyes away and refocused on her large duffel bags. "I'm packing."

"Moving out are you?"

"Yes. You know that."

"Do I? Oh, I must've forgotten." She was teasing her and Jude knew it.

"Is there something I can help you with?" She placed her bags on the floor and walked toward her. She looked deadly in her worn jeans, dark, heavy boots, and a black tank. Mary could've come on the spot, especially when Jude's wicked gold eyes flicked at her just like they did that very first night.

"Yes, I think there might be." She held her ground even when Jude was a short breath away. "I'm looking for a teacher."

"Oh?"

"Yes, someone who can teach me a bit of German. Know anyone?"

"I might."

"She has to be good-looking, though. Gorgeous, in fact. With a jawline like a god and hard-edged muscles."

Jude leaned in.

"And blond. She has to have short blond hair, and—"

But Jude cut her off, lifting her quickly and pinning her to the wall. She kissed her wildly. Mary had to turn away to speak, and it was still difficult with Jude rubbing against her and sucking on her neck.

"And she has to be tall and strong and confident. And—"

Jude kissed her again and lowered her a bit to fumble in Mary's purse. When she found what she was looking for, she grabbed it and then flung the purse to the floor.

"What are you—" Mary couldn't quite see what Jude was doing; she could only feel and then Jude was pressing against her tightly, holding her up with her body while her hand messed with her jeans. As soon as Mary realized what she was doing, Jude had shoved up her skirt and was positioning the phallus at her opening and then—

Jude thrust and Mary flung her head back and cried out short and sharp.

"Jude!"

"Yes, baby, take it."

"Oh God. Oh God. It feels so good." She ran her hands over her face and kissed her deeply as Jude continued to shove into her. "Jude, oh fuck, baby." She clawed at her back and hair, held on to her neck as the thrusting grew more frenzied.

"Jude, Jude," she said, closing her eyes to the onset of pleasure. "Jude, Jude, Jude!" And she came with her body tensing against Jude, pushing back on her, legs flexed, toes pointed, arms squeezing Jude tightly. It went on and on and Jude never stopped. She just kept thrusting and pushing, until Mary went hoarse and limp in her arms.

They both struggled to breathe, and eventually Jude lowered them both as she eased to her knees. Her neck and face were red with exertion, her veins thick with rushing blood. Mary nibbled on one running along her shoulder.

"Jude?" She smelled of sweat and that same masculine cologne.

"Yes?"

"Remember when I told you I didn't want to scare you?"

Jude searched her eyes.

"Well, I think I should tell you."

"Tell me what?"

She looked so raw with desire and spent energy.

"I love you."

Jude stared at her, but Mary could tell the words had reached her. Her eyes were churning like a glowing pot of honey.

"I'm in love with you," Mary whispered. She touched her face. "Am I scaring you?"

"No, not at all."

Mary sighed and laughed nervously. "Good. I was afraid you might want to run."

Jude took her hand and kissed it. "I—"

"You don't have to say anything. I didn't say it so you would—"

"Shh." Jude pressed a finger to her lips. "I'm in love with you too."

"You are?"

"Yes."

"Are you sure?"

Jude laughed. "I am. But—"

"But what?" Her heart raced with panic.

"I love you, Mary, but you talk too much." She laughed and kissed her, squeezing her buttocks. "Way too much."

"Oh, I do, do I?"

"Yes."

Mary pushed away, laughing when Jude held fast to her, trying to kiss her. She managed to stand and gain her balance. Jude's laughter died as Mary retrieved her purse.

"You're leaving?"

"No. But—"

"But what?" Jude stood. Her confidence had returned, and Mary had to look away so she could concentrate on what she was looking for. When she found it in the bottom of her purse, she smiled devilishly at Jude.

"But there's something I wanted to do before we left this place for good."

"Really." She nodded. Jude inched closer. "Well, what is it?"

"Are you sure you're ready for it?"

"I'm sure."

"You have to be really sure. And if you want me to stop you have to say stop. No other—"

Jude pressed her finger to her lips again. "Zip it and tell me, Mary." She tugged on her lips with her hot mouth. "I won't need you to stop."

Mary held up the handcuffs and swung them on her finger.

Jude laughed and tried to take them.

"Oh, no," Mary said. "These are going on you, my love."

"You really think so?"

"I know so."

"You're going to have to make me," Jude said, serious with need and desire.

Mary tossed her purse aside and moved toward her. "Oh, I plan on it."

THE END

About the Author

Ronica Black is an award winning author and a three-time Lambda Literary Finalist. Her books range from romance and erotica to mystery and intrigue, and she enjoys trying her hand at all. Her next book, *Wholehearted*, a traditional romance, is to be published in 2012. Ronica also enjoys drawing, painting, and sculpting. She lives in Glendale, Arizona, with her partner where she relishes a rich family life and raising a menagerie of pets.

Books Available From Bold Strokes Books

Wild by Meghan O'Brien. Shapeshifter Selene Rhodes dreads the full moon and the loss of control it brings, but when she rescues forensic pathologist Eve Thomas from a vicious attack by a masked man, she discovers that she isn't the scariest monster in San Francisco. (978-1-60282-227-6)

Reluctant Hope by Erin Dutton. Cancer survivor Addison Hunt knows she can't offer any guarantees, in love or in life, and after experiencing a loss of her own, Brooke Donahue isn't willing to risk her heart. (978-1-60282-228-3)

Conquest by Ronica Black. When Mary Brunelle stumbles into the arms of Jude Jaeger, a gorgeous dominatrix at a private night club, Mary is smitten, but she soon finds out Jude is her professor, and Professor Jaeger doesn't date her students...or her conquests. (978-1-60282-229-0)

The Affair of the Porcelain Dog by Jess Farady. What darkness stalks the London streets at night? Ira Adler, present plaything of crime lord Cain Goddard, will soon find out. (978-1-60282-230-6)

365 Days by KE Payne. What do you do when you're fifteen years old, confused about your sexuality, and the girl of your dreams doesn't even know you exist? Clemmie has 365 days to discover for herself, and she's going to have a blast doing it! (978-1-60282-540-6)

Darkness Embraced by Winter Pennington. Surrounded by harsh vampire politics and secret ambitions, Epiphany learns that an old enemy is plotting treason against the woman she once loved, and to save all she holds dear, she must embrace and form an alliance with the dark. (978-1-60282-221-4)

78 Keys by Kristin Marra. When the cosmic powers choose Devorah Rosten to be their next gladiator, she must use her unique skills to try to save her lover, herself, and even humankind. (978-1-60282-222-1)

Playing Passion's Game by Lesley Davis. Trent Williams's only passion in life is gaming—until Juliet Sullivan makes her realize that love can be a whole different game to play. (978-1-60282-223-8)

Retirement Plan by Martha Miller. A modern morality tale of justice, retribution, and women who refuse to be politely invisible. (978-1-60282-224-5)

Who Dat Whodunnit by Greg Herren. Popular New Orleans detective Scotty Bradley investigates the murder of a dethroned beauty queen to clear the name of his pro football–playing cousin. (978-1-60282-225-2)

The Company He Keeps by Dale Chase. A riotously erotic collection of stories set in the sexually repressed and therefore sexually rampant Victorian era. (978-1-60282-226-9)

Cursebusters! by Julie Smith. Budding-psychic Reeno is the most accomplished teenage burglar in California, but one tiny screw-up and poof!—she's sentenced to Bad Girl School. And that isn't even her worst problem. Her sister Haley's dying of an illness no one can diagnose, and now she can't even help. (978-1-60282-559-8)

True Confessions by PJ Trebelhorn. Lynn Patrick finally has a chance with the only woman she's ever loved, her lifelong friend Jessica Greenfield, but Jessie is still tormented by an abusive past. (978-1-60282-216-0)

Jane Doe by Lisa Girolami. On a getaway trip to Las Vegas, Emily Carver gambles on a chance for true love and discovers that sometimes in order to find yourself, you have to start from scratch. (978-1-60282-217-7)

Ghosts of Winter by Rebecca S. Buck. Can Ros Wynne, who has lost everything she thought defined her, find her true life—and her true love—surrounded by the lingering history of the once-grand Winter Manor? (978-1-60282-219-1)

Who I Am by M.L. Rice. Devin Kelly's senior year is a disaster. She's in a new school in a new town, and the school bully is making her life miserable—but then she meets his sister Melanie and realizes her feelings for her are more than platonic. (978-1-60282-231-3)

Call Me Softly by D. Jackson Leigh. Polo pony trainer Swain Butler finds that neither her heart nor her secret are safe when beautiful British heiress Lillie Wetherington arrives to bury her grandmother, Swain's employer. (978-1-60282-215-3)

Split by Mel Bossa. Weeks before Derek O'Reilly's engagement party, a chance meeting with Nick Lund, his teenage first love, catapults him into the past, where he relives that powerful relationship revealing what he and Nick were, still are, and might yet be to each other. (978-1-60282-220-7)

Blood Hunt by L.L. Raand. In the second Midnight Hunters Novel, Detective Jody Gates, heir to a powerful Vampire clan, forges an uneasy alliance with Sylvan, the wolf Were Alpha, to battle a shadow army of humans and rogue Weres, while fighting her growing hunger for human reporter Becca Land. (978-1-60282-209-2)

Loving Liz by Bobbi Marolt. When theater actor Marty Jamison turns diva and Liz Chandler walks out on her, Marty must confront a cheating lover from the past to understand why life is crumbling around her. (978-1-60282-210-8)

Kiss the Rain by Larkin Rose. How will successful fashion designer Eve Harris react when she discovers the new woman in her life, Jodi, and her secret fantasy phone date, Lexi, are one and the same? (978-1-60282-211-5)

Sarah, Son of God by Justine Saracen. In a story within a story within a story, a transgendered beauty takes us through Stonewall-rioting New York, Venice under the Inquisition, and Nero's Rome. (978-1-60282-212-2)

Sleeping Angel by Greg Herren. Eric Matthews survives a terrible car accident only to find out everyone in town thinks he's a murderer—and he has to clear his name even though he has no memories of what happened. (978-1-60282-214-6)